VESNA MAIN was born in Zagreb, Croatia. She is a
graduate in comparative literature and has a PhD from the
Shakespeare Institute, University of Birmingham. She was
a lecturer at universities in Nigeria and the UK and worked
for the BBC. Her articles, reviews and short stories have
appeared in newspapers and literary journals. Her published
novels are *A Woman With No Clothes On* (Delancey
Press, 2008) and *The Reader the Writer* (Mirador, 2015).

VESNA MAIN

TEMPTATION

A USER'S GUIDE

SALT

LONDON

PUBLISHED BY SALT PUBLISHING 2017

2 4 6 8 10 9 7 5 3 1

Copyright © Vesna Main 2018

First published in Great Britain in 2018 by
Salt Publishing Ltd
International House, 24 Holborn Viaduct, London EC1A 2BN United Kingdom

www.saltpublishing.com

Salt Publishing Limited Reg. No. 5293401

A CIP catalogue record for this book is available from the British Library

ISBN 978 1 78463 128 4 (Paperback edition)
ISBN 978 1 78463 129 1 (Electronic edition)

Typeset in Neacademia by Salt Publishing

Printed and bound in Great Britain by Clays Ltd, St Ives plc

In memory of my parents,
and my friends Manuel Alvarado,
David Potter and Max Lab

Contents

'It is strange that no reader ever understood that my only subject is love.'

ALBERTO MANGUEL, *All Men Are Liars*

Safe

I T WAS HER time now. She was safe. She could leave. No one would stop her. She doesn't have to see him again. She knew all that and yet the voice kept repeating the same thing. But something else, not a voice, a force inside her wouldn't let go. That force made her fetch a knife from a drawer in the kitchen. That force made her walk back to the room. That force made her push the blade into Dave, lying sprawled on the floor, snoring. As the steel cut into his chest, he jumped, startled, uttered a cry, of shock or anger – she couldn't tell. Fear ripped his eyes open. He lurched to one side, shaking, trying to grab her, mad from pain. But he was drunk with beer and sleep and she was quicker. She stabbed him again. And then she stabbed Marvin and saw his kind, lined face grimace with pain. And again. And again she had it for Dave. Quick, sharp stabs. In out, faster and faster, like someone going mad chopping onions. Each time she shoved home the knife, his blood spurted its red warmth onto her face, onto her half-naked body, onto the walls around them. It dripped on the carpet; she could feel its drying stickiness on the skin between her toes. Her hand moved as if someone was directing it, pushing it with a long stick as if she were a puppet. And the hand carried on working for a long time after he had stopped making any sound. All she could hear was the swish as the knife passed through his chest. When she stopped, she was gasping for breath. The swish continued. His body lay next to her like a huge wet sponge. The hard work was over. She could relax. She fell backwards into an armchair, her legs stretched out. She had no energy left, her body a rag doll. If he could get up now, she wouldn't be able to fight back. She was certain of that. But he was more dead than the corpses she had seen on the telly. She closed her eyes. She was safe. It was her time now.

She must have dozed off. When she woke up, the blood on her skin had dried. There was daylight and the sun hurt her eyes. Her body shivered with cold. She screamed when she saw him: his eyes bulging like in a horror film. She rushed out of the room. Was he still alive?

She should wash her hands, her body, the carpet, the walls. And him? If he were dead, she could take him somewhere. Hide him. But she wouldn't do any of that. She had killed him. She was going to jail. And then she saw him, a big body stumbling towards her, his eyes bleeding sockets. But the face was kind, the face of Marvin, lined. He was smiling, putting out his hand towards her, checking that her body was warm. Marvin, her mother's friend, who bought her ice-cream, who made sure that she was warm inside and down there. Marvin was kind. But his fingers were cold, bony, an old person's fingers. Not like Dave's, Dave's fingers chubby like sausages. Marvin was kind. Kind to her. Kind to her mother. Why was his face the same as Dave's? She grabbed her coat and ran into the street. She ran, her bare feet slapping the cold tarmac. Dave lumbered after her. She ran until she couldn't see him. But she knew he would come and she was scared.

She banged on the door of a house. She banged and called until a window opened in a room upstairs. And another one in the neighbouring house. A door unlocked and she rushed in. The rest happened to someone else and she watched it from the side without feeling a thing. People in the house, a police ride, a station, questions – she couldn't tell what they had to do with her – but the questions, so many questions and a doctor who came to examine her for wounds, samples of blood they took and then a shower. She sat on a cracked tiled floor and let the water run over her head, over her hunched body. She saw herself jumping away from Dave as he pulled off her bra and threw it to Nige. She crossed her arms to cover her naked breasts. Nige sniffed her bra. The other man was laughing loudly and banging his fist on his knee. 'Come on, give us a bit of fun,' Dave said, 'a bit more, the last bit.' He tugged at her knickers. Nige had his hand in his trousers and the other man had unzipped himself and was rubbing his cock. Dave pushed her onto the sofa between the two men and then Nige pulled her on top of him. Gavin was next to him. She felt them pull off her knickers. She lashed out, kicking and scratching. It was this or she was nothing. She howled and bit whoever came near. Nige was swearing, mad with pain and anger: 'Fucking bitch, you'll pay for this.' She screamed as he hit her on her face and breasts and forced himself inside her. The other man was holding her legs apart. She went on screaming and scratching and eventually the two men left her alone. 'Can't you shut the bitch up?' Gavin shouted to Dave. 'You need to learn to control your missus,' Nige said. The water became cold but she sat there letting it run over her bare back until someone came and put a towel over her.

They told her he was dead and she neither believed nor disbelieved them. It didn't matter. She was safe. And she wondered whether she had died because everything was different and she was different. She had to be dead. Alive, she had felt that force taking over her and then there were things she loved and things she hated, but now it was all the same. The next day she was in a holding cell when a man came to see her and said he was her lawyer. He was there to help her and he talked and talked. And that same question that the police had asked.

When she had returned from the refuge Dave had been nice, had bought stuff from Iceland and they had tea like a proper couple. He didn't mind when she wanted to see *EastEnders*. He made fun of the story and laughed as he talked about the cleavage of one of the women but that was all right. And then one evening, as she was about to put burgers under the grill, there was a knock on the door and it was Gavin. He had broken down not far from their place and he wanted Dave to help him. She wanted to go with them – she didn't care about missing *EastEnders* – but Dave said she should stay and watch the telly. He said he wouldn't be long. But he was. She was asleep when he returned. She remembered him drunk, pushing himself into her.

'But why didn't you leave?' He didn't listen. Did he want her to repeat it?

The evenings after that followed the same pattern: Dave went out, usually with Gavin and came back drunk. Sometimes, when he was on an afternoon shift, Gavin came over with beer and they would drink before lunch. After Dave had turned up for work drunk for the second time, they sacked him. Of course they did; he was a driver for an off licence and they were strict about such things. Then he started complaining about her not working. She had tried hard, in shops and bars, but there was nothing or else the money was shit – it was better to be on the dole – and every day they argued. He said she should go back on the street but she didn't want to do that any more. He hit her. Once when they quarrelled, the neighbours called the police but all the police did was to tell them to quieten down. That same evening he beat her up so badly that she lost consciousness.

The lawyer interrupted again with that same question: 'Why didn't you leave him?'

She thought for a long time but couldn't think what to say. He was her man, it was proper; it wasn't like Marvin giving money to her mother, it was real, they had dated for real. She wanted to stick with Dave. She could see it wasn't easy for him with no money and no job. She had to help him out. That's what couples did. And he was sorry when he hit her. Sometimes he said so.

'Tits, give us the tits, come on.' That was Nige's voice. And then Gavin echoing him: 'Tits, tits.' She saw herself moving towards the door. But as she turned around, Dave was standing next to her. He took her in his arms and started to dance. It was nice. The men laughed and clapped. Then Dave kissed her and, for a moment, she thought he was thanking her and she would be free to go. She relaxed and let him turn her around, but he surprised her by unclasping her bra. Nige and the other man shouted: 'Yes, tits, get her here.'

'But you could have walked out? You chose not to,' the lawyer said.

It was early afternoon when he came home with Gavin and Nige, carrying six-packs. He pushed her into the bedroom and closed the door: 'Look, help me out. Nige has promised me a job.' He spoke quietly, as if not wanting the others to hear. 'A proper job.' She didn't believe him. He said: 'Nige's brother-in-law is opening a bar and needs a bouncer; I could fix things for him, be around. I have to keep him sweet.' She asked what he wanted her to do. 'A slow dance, and strip a bit . . . put them in good mood . . . that's all.' She stared at him. Three men drinking together and her stripping. That won't be all. She didn't do that any more.

'Look, Tan, you don't want to work.'

'I do. I'll get something. They promised me,' she said.

'Oh, they promised you,' he mocked. 'And you believed them.' He turned away from her, lit a cigarette. 'Have you forgotten Lilla?' he shouted. 'If I had a job, you could look after her, be a proper mum. I'm doing it for both of us.' He sat on the bed, smoking, staring at her. She turned away, looked out of the window. The back yard was paved; that was where they kept the bins and Dave's broken motorbike. She remembered when he tried to repair it and couldn't and made it worse. That was the day when she was cheated and taken to that house. She had agreed to do a job in a car and then there were three men and they had raped her. They didn't even pay and then Dave had hit her when she got home with no money. But it was the motorbike he was really angry about.

The question again, that question she had come to dread. He was thick, this lawyer.

'Tan, come here, babe.' He patted the bed next to him. She didn't trust him, but she obeyed. 'Come on, sit down.' He put his arm around her, kissed her on the cheek and whispered into her ear. 'It's all right, if you don't want to help. But . . . I need work . . . and it's fucking hard to get anything. Nige has promised. I could start next week. That's why I got the beer . . . to celebrate.' He ran the back of his hand across her cheek. 'You get my drift?' He kissed her on the mouth.

'Only stripping, no more?'

'Yeah, of course.'

'Only the shirt and skirt off. I can keep the bra and knickers on, yeah?'

'Yeah, whatever.' He stood up. She wanted to help him but she wasn't going further. She'd do the dance and nothing else. Dave walked out. Through the closed door, she heard him talking to his friends and them laughing loudly.

'Stripping for three drunk men? In your home? That's mad. You were asking for it.' This lawyer was doing her head in. Why was he so stupid? It was only a little strip, nothing else. Helping out.

A few minutes later, one of them shouted: 'Show! When's the show starting?' She heard clapping and cheering. She wanted to tell Dave she was afraid they expected more than a strip. She heard him call: 'Come on, Tan babe, we're waiting.' He wasn't angry.

She opened the door and walked in. Dave had already moved the coffee table to the side and she stepped onto the rug in the middle of the room. Nige and Gavin were slumped on the sofa, beer cans in their hands. Dave sat in the armchair. The stereo was playing. She got on with it straightaway, thinking that the sooner she started, the sooner it would be over. It was important to please Dave by pleasing the men, but she was wary of getting them excited. They leered at her and she hated that. But it would be all over soon. She made herself think it was somebody else stripping, not her. Her mind was on that Great Yarmouth promenade, breeze in her hair, the ice-cream van playing a jingle. Marvin holding her hand. She unbuttoned her shirt slowly, but made sure that her eyes did not meet the men's. With each button she unfastened, the men cheered. Then she took off her shoes, one by one, and the tights – she had she'd had no time to put on stockings – caressing her legs, as if trying to memorise their shape. She moved around, wriggling her hips, dancing barefoot in her skirt and bra. Nige tried to touch her but she managed to move away and he mumbled, 'Teasing bitch.' She went on dancing, but the other man shouted 'Skirt off, skirt off' and she began to tug at the zip, pulling it down and then a little bit up until it was done. She took off the skirt as slowly as she could and then carried on dancing. That was that. No more.

'But even then you could have walked out.' What was he saying?

Gavin pulled her knickers off and forced himself inside her, Nige doing the same from the back. She fought them, biting and scratching, that force inside her giving her strength, incredible strength. They were shouting 'Shut the bitch up' and running out, running away from her.

'Your story's no good. You consented. Why didn't you leave?' the lawyer asked.

Dave was furious, strode towards her, but she was quicker. She locked herself in the bathroom. And then it was quiet. She didn't know how it happened but soon he was asleep. No, she is sure he wasn't dead. She heard him snoring.

'And then? He woke up and attacked you with a knife and you had to defend yourself,' the lawyer said.

No, she was sure that he didn't. He wouldn't have done that. He was a fist man, not a knife man. Besides, he was too drunk and when he fell it was like he had passed out. In a second, he was fast asleep. But she was very angry with him. Mad at him. That mad like when you think I could kill that person, I could chop them up into tiny bits. But when she went to fetch the knife she wasn't thinking that. She wasn't thinking anything. She was only doing things. No, that's not

8

true. Her body was moving on its own. Her hand grabbed the knife and pushed it inside his chest and out.

The lawyer said that what she had just said didn't sound right and that she was in trouble if she stuck to the story. He said that it didn't happen like that. She was a confused young woman. What did he mean? He was going to write down what happened and she would sign it and then say the same to the police. Why was he asking her then if he knew what had happened? She said it loudly but he didn't answer. Instead, he repeated that she had killed her violent boyfriend in self-defence. He wrote that down into his notebook. But was it Dave or was it Marvin who was dead, Marvin with his kind, lined face? The lawyer stared at her before repeating that it was Dave who had fetched the knife from a kitchen drawer and who had tried to stab her but she had fought him and killed him in self-defence. But what about Marvin? He was checking that she was warm. It was self-defence, she had to remember that. She didn't care either way. She had told him what it was like – she knew, she watched it happen – but if he wanted to believe something else, it was none of her business. She was fine. That force had let go of her. She was safe.

A Woman With No Clothes On

WHEN EDOUARD INVITED me for a picnic, I suspected ulterior motives. I said yes, on condition he paints a picture based on my idea. I visualised a woman, with no clothes on, sharing a basket lunch with two men. The male figures would have to be fully clothed, the brown of their jackets blending with the surroundings. I wanted the woman to be the focus of the viewer's gaze and it was essential that she returned that gaze as boldly as she could, transforming herself from an object to a subject in control. In my mind, I heard the men discussing some eternal truth, or a myth, perhaps suggested by a classical figure sketched in the background, enveloped in a gauzy garment, looking away from the scene. The woman with no clothes on, the naked woman, not a nude goddess, she would impart the idea of being here and now, a contemporary figure, almost falling out of the canvas, transcending the boundary between the world of the painting and the world of the Paris in 1860s. It was essential that she existed in the viewer's present.

I knew Edouard was lonely – no wonder, he couldn't tolerate fools; besides, he was often moody, troubled by something indefinable – and infatuated with me. I could ask for anything. He listened carefully to my idea and nodded, slowly and gently, as if he were transported to the picture that was emerging in his head.

I did not mind staying a night at the studio. He sketched

tirolosoly and said he would require me to return to pose when he was ready to work with oils.

The painting was turned down for the 1863 Salon. Exhibited at the Salon des Refusés, it became the talk of the town.

My idea became the talk of the town.

Mrs Dalloway

'THE MARQUISE WENT out at five o'clock,' Colin says but no one hears. His sentence, for ever his, all that story-telling and whodunnit has never interested her. A week before finals, when she had given him Barthes and had read out the sentence, he had said, 'That's how I shall begin.' She didn't ask what he meant; too busy studying with him every day and late into the night that week. Not that he had done much before; he didn't mind getting a 2:1. She would have been distraught. 'To A, who gave me the first sentence' came a few months after graduation. 'He was in love with you. And still is,' Richard said later, years later. 'Why else would he dedicate his first novel to you?' Wrong as usual, poor Richard. How little he knows people.

'The marquise went out at five. Why not the duchess? Why not at six?' Emilie teased him, Emilie, the first woman who recognised the words. 'The only woman I can marry, don't you think, Anna?' As if she had to approve Colin's girlfriend. Did he mean it as a test, a test for his future wife or a provocation for her, for her who was already married? Emilie passed, being French, would have read Valéry. The reviewers didn't get it, too obscure for them, even then, thirty years ago. Much worse these days, all hacks. Agents wouldn't pick it up either. Commercial gatekeepers. Some, maybe. Order in stories, she had to explain to Richard. Yes, the marquise, not the duchess, and at five, definitely not at six. Order in stories but chance

in life. Is that the beauty of it? Or not? The beauty of what?
Stories or life?

'The traffic's hopeless,' Marc says, justifying his lateness, or
maybe to support Richard. Male solidarity. His usual party
piece. 'I was stuck on Hammersmith Bridge for three quarters
of an hour . . .' After twenty-odd years in London, he ought to
be used to it. That candle, she needs to move it . . . yes, that's
better. As Richard says, what's stopping him moving out? Not
a steady job, that's for sure. He could do his art anywhere, if
only he bothered to pick up a brush. He claims the muse has
left him. Nonsense. He's lazy, that's all there is to it. Why is
he moving the candle back? She hates symmetry on the table.
It's her dinner party. If only he would take a breath between
sentences, others might be able to join the conversation. He's
a friend, an old friend, and she loves him but she can't allow
him to dominate. Richard must be fed up too. No wonder
he seems to have switched off. That's what he does with her
and then he has no idea, accuses her of not telling him. The
others must be bored as well. Really, Marc's monopolising her
party. But is Richard subdued? Or tired after a long meeting.
Could he be upset with her? She had been worried and she
had lots to do; he should understand how she felt. It's not as
if she didn't remind him in the morning and then he said he
would be home earlier to help. She counted on him, of course,
she did. All right, it wasn't much fun for him either, enduring
Bob's blathering – there's something about that man, he's all
over the place, with his baggy trousers, no one else wears
anything like them, and the way he throws his legs about
as if he had two left feet, a total mess, no wonder he can't
keep to the agenda – but then it's not only him, all his staff,
and that Myra, they all babble, their meetings go on for ever.

Richard's colleagues must be the most tedious academics in the country. They need somebody in control, but not Bob, that's for sure. Bob who insists on chairing every meeting. But Richard could have rung. Maybe not. It might have been one of those situations where you think it's about to end, it's not worth ringing, but then it goes on and on and each time you think that's it. Before you know it, hours have passed. It's happened to her. Well, not quite hours but . . . It can make you tense. He would have been anxious.

'Richard, you were stuck as well?' Marc says.

'No, no. It wasn't the traffic.' So dismissive of Marc's question, so jittery.

'What I'm saying, London's too big . . .' Will he go on about town planners next, like last time? Then Charles will feel obliged to start his own spiel. Let's not have a repeat. Boring it was. Good for people to talk, but Marc's obsessed. Richard is eating slowly, his eyes on the plate. If only she hadn't said those things. She can't help thinking the worst. Other people don't immediately imagine tube bombs and heart attacks. She shouldn't have been so harsh. But why didn't he explain what kept him? The way he stood behind Marc, who was doing his round of greetings, histrionic, kissing and hugging her. Hello darling, you look fantastic. Carrying a board game, quite absurd. Always a big entrance, like an actor. Did he think this was a children's do? She must have made a face . . . and why not? He ought to know she hates board games. Is there anything sillier? And there was Richard, stooped, clasping his hands in front of him, as if he were in short trousers waiting to be told off by the headmaster. Marc can intimidate people but Richard was on his own ground, and yet he had that air of self-consciousness, inexcusable in anyone above thirty. It didn't help when Colin made the joke about two lads together somewhere secret and Marc winked at him, going along with it – now that was too much – and everyone laughed, but Richard looked down. Did he blush? No, he couldn't have, she must have imagined it. She was irritated with him and marched off to the kitchen. He followed her and she told him that he had let her down. Not straightaway, no. She waited for him to explain why he was late. But not a word. That made it worse: he could see something was wrong and yet he didn't offer an apology or explanation for his part. Why not, why couldn't he have done that? She would have understood. But he was all silence. That was why she blew up. And then she was cold, she brushed him off. If only she could give him a hug now. When they are alone, he will complain to her about Colin's sexist joke. Two of you lads being somewhere secret. As if she were responsible for her friends. Yes, sexist, but Colin's like that. There he is: taking Christina's hand and running his finger over her palm, tracing her lines, like a fortune-teller. The way he is looking into her eyes; but they're old friends. And now he is whispering into her ear, what a performance. Poor Christina probably hasn't had so much male attention in years; Charles always seems so distant. Must be nice being married to an architect, not having to think about the house, all the little decisions one has to make taken care of; she would have liked that, but Charles, Charles is too distant. She couldn't cope with someone like him. It would make her feel unloved. Poor Christina. She isn't taking her hand away. Yes, Colin's a flirt but that doesn't mean he has a roving eye. Richard's silly to be jealous – for that's what it is – of anyone who knew her before him, even friends. Colin likes people; he is friendly, chatty. Richard wouldn't understand.

Colin's interested in others; what writer isn't? But Emilie's safe with him. Thirty years she has known him. She would vouch for him. And for Richard. Well, anyone would vouch for Richard.

Poor him. She won't tell him what happened when Colin and Emilie arrived. He would only spin a story about Colin's infidelities being the cause of the tension. Laughable how little he understands others. She could tell something wasn't quite right. Emilie sounded hostile – as never before – when Colin ranted about mock Tudor houses. He hates them. So does she. Anyone with visual sense does. But the way Emilie frowned, quite unlike her. After more than ten years of marriage, she knows he's an architect manqué. They must have had a disagreement earlier on. Couples have them. But she and Richard wouldn't have behaved like that in front of others. It made her uncomfortable; no wonder she knocked over the bottle of wine. There's still a small stain on the hem of her dress. What if it doesn't come out? She will take it to the cleaners tomorrow. There is a specialist one, good with delicate materials, but no, they're closed for a week, Seychelles or something like that, she heard. She would hate to see the dress ruined.

'More salad?'

Emilie nods.

'Shall I serve you, *ma chérie*?' Marc says.

'More wine?' Richard should be topping up. Still looking down, unwilling to play the host. The lines around his eyes. Still at the meeting? Pity he can't relax. Marc has been making up for him; that must come from living alone. But not for Sarah and it's four years now. Almost. A cold November day. The sun shining. Was it Manet who said he wouldn't allow funerals when the sun shone? Remembers that when she sees a funeral. And the image of Manet walking behind Delacroix's coffin, at Père Lachaise, a warm, sunny day. Four years ago for Jocelyn, that brilliant light, the crisp air, the firm, frosty ground around the crematorium. The music was uplifting, You would expect a musician to pick up stuff like that. All planned as soon as the prognosis came. How does Sarah manage? No one since Jocelyn, four years now. She couldn't bear to be unloved, not for that long, not for four months. No wonder Sarah's gloomy.

Richard's pouring more wine into his glass. How many has he had? Too many. Oh, she didn't mean it. She blows up but that's the end of it. He shouldn't feel hurt for ever. Has he got the habit? Wine every day. He could be the type, him with his little obsessions. The way he goes on with his little routines. He should have been an accountant, not a historian, not an academic. She mustn't let him drink too much. This studious look becomes him; more appealing now that his hair has gone grey. She couldn't be in love with a man who has no focus, something artistic, intellectual. That's why Marc isn't attractive. Too lukewarm about art, too jaded. Why does it happen? She won't allow it to happen to her, or to Richard. Marc's boring. She couldn't find him attractive. But Richard has always had it. The passion in his voice when he talked about Annie, the working class suffragette, Annie Kenney, was it? The morning, or was it the afternoon, in front of the library? She knew she could love him, and it's still there, his passion, and her love. After all these years. Twenty-five. Pity he can be so conventional. His shock when she said they should sneak upstairs for a few minutes, for a quick screw, like that couple in the Buñuel film. He walked away without a word. Poor Richard.

'Yes, we're leaving next week,' Emilie says.

'I envy you. How long are you staying?'

'Six months, maybe more.'

'What about work?'

'Unpaid leave. Easy to get a French assistant. The French are queueing to come over.'

'Lucky you. Last year New York,' Christina says. 'I wish I could travel.'

'Colin needs peace to work and, for me, I want to be closer to my parents; my mother needs moral support. My father had a heart attack.'

Richard should have a check-up. Men over fifty get heart attacks. He has been putting on weight. It can't be the food; he doesn't eat more than before. It's the drink, the lack of exercise. She is lucky; well, not quite, her tummy muscles aren't as taut as they used to be. Must use that rolling wheel. Something's bothering him. Can't be sulking because of her; he wouldn't do that in public. Soon, as soon as the gallery business settles a bit, she'll spend more time with him. They could go away for a week, or a long weekend. Oh God, no, she doesn't want to think about it now. Sarah. Would the others have heard? The door of the lounge was closed. How could she? Well, they both screamed. And that bumblebee, the bloody thing kept crashing into the lamp. Did it come in with her? No, it couldn't have. It's been too cold, too wet. Stupid thing. And then, when she went back to the kitchen and Richard followed, the blasted thing made its final, suicidal dash. Lying dead on the floor. In the lounge they sensed something, something in the tone of their voices, something delicate was abroad. Christina hugged and kissed Sarah, gently, as if she needed protecting. Were they feeling sorry? Embarrassed?

'The food's lovely,' Emilie says. Kind Emilie. 'The artichokes are heavenly. Which mushrooms did you use?' How
effortlessly stylish she looks. Parisian women: they simply have
it. The picture when she opened the door. A truly beautiful
picture. A good start for her party, that's what she thought.
Both of them dressed in black, chic, Colin held an armful
of white tulips – her favourite, except in springtime, when
she prefers yellow flowers – framed by the doorway. 'Don't
move.' She wanted to prolong that moment of beauty and
Colin frowned. 'Why not, why can't we move?' That was it.
Gone, that fleeting moment was gone, the flowers withered,
the clothes changed colour. Gone for ever. She knew then, she
knew something wasn't right between them. Let them not be
miserable at her party. Or argue. When she told them about
the beautiful image they presented, he laughed, but not nicely.
A nervous laugh. 'Silly, silly as always, Anna.' Unkind, yes,
dismissive of her, critical, as if she had been trivial. She's a
gallery owner, for God's sake, she has to be visual. Emilie told
him not to be rude. She looked serious, angry. A bad start, she
knew it then. And then Sarah, and Richard, her two screaming
matches. Fine now. Good food makes a difference.

She had to take the afternoon off. Absolutely. If you cut
corners . . . it shows. She likes everything to be in order, the
house tidy and welcoming, no lingering smells, all the prepa-
rations completed, the table set, attractive. The white roses
look lovely, tightly bunched together, their stalks cut short and
buds half open. Only one florist does it like this. Right for the
table. French, the woman is, certainly. Calls her madame. A
lovely accent, stronger than Emilie's. A tall bouquet blocks eye
contact. Not the worst. Gosh, some people. That couple from
the local Humanist Society, still flicking through a recipe book

as their guests were arriving. No sense of urgency. Could not agree on the choice of dish. A thick soup using everything they could find in the vegetable rack. Everyone starving. And then ice cream, industrial, not organic. A mess around. Everyone helping. Slack people. 'Homely. Relaxed. Lovely,' Richard said. 'The Dunkirk spirit and jolly chaos bringing people together.' He who is so proper laughed it off. He who cares about the etiquette of the placements for cutlery, how could he think that the house was cosy and lived in? What a stupid phrase that is, an excuse for mess. Lived in, indeed. He wanted to wind her up. Wouldn't miss an opportunity to make fun of her tidiness, like some rebellious teenager. But that evening still gives her nightmares. She's the host and the guests are arriving, nothing's ready, she's running around, starting different tasks, unable to complete any of them, something's holding her back, she can't tell what, she can't do anything, the guests are ringing the bell . . .

'Anna mentioned you had some new stuff for the archives?' Colin says. He must have noted Richard's elsewhere. Difficult not to, you don't have to be a writer, you don't need honed observational skills to notice something's bugging Richard. Okay, he didn't help, he was late but now that he's here, he ought to make an effort. She wanted this evening to be special. It's been in the offing for months. Whenever she fixed a date, someone couldn't make it, and she wanted them all here together, sharing food, wine, good conversation. The recipe for the main course – she had never done it before – was fiddly, she took her time, you can't rush these things – but it's worked. Porcini, good-quality porcini. Powerful flavour. Artichokes tend to be bland. Pity the bread wasn't in the oven when the guests arrived; the smell of freshly baking bread is welcoming. You should have it in when potential buyers visit. Or is it coffee? Both? It doesn't matter. A silly gimmick. They aren't selling the house.

Are the glasses in the right order? Where do you put a water glass? To the left or right of the one for white wine? And is that to the left of the red? Three glasses, many permutations. He'd tell her off if wrong. She forgets such things, but why shouldn't she? They don't matter, silly conventions; more important to get the visual impact and that's nothing to do with rules, with the etiquette of laying the table.

Food, however, that's a different matter. Food's important to her. Her identity, some of it, comes from her attitude to food, not eating food, it's preparing, offering that matters. She reads recipes for pleasure, she makes up new dishes, she loves cooking, cooking for others, for her friends, family. The girls used to tease her . . . a Jewish mother, offering food, and she was not even Jewish.

'That chap of yours, the funny one in baggy corduroys, the head of department,' Charles says, addressing Richard, 'was at RIBA this afternoon for a reception.'

Richard frowns.

'You introduced me once. We nodded at each other but I had to move on. Forgot his name.'

Bob? Not possible. Richard complained Bob was awful at the meeting. Charles must be wrong but it's rude of Richard to ignore him.

Now Sarah's turning to Richard, united, for once, by a common foe, the two subdued ones. She is sulking, avoiding her eyes. She might have meant well, but, really, she has overstepped the mark this time. Signing a contract, behind her back, at that percentage. Could it still be valid? Probably. But she won't make a fuss. Let it go. As long as it doesn't happen again. To engage a new artist – true, the one she found and wanted – without proper consultation and at that percentage. What does she think she's doing? Since Jocelyn, it's not been easy. But she can't expect others always to be making allowances. All this excessive care for her mother and taking the reins at the gallery. Trying to fill the gap in her life. Needs a focus – some people get a cat, oh but Sarah hates cats – fair enough, but she can't behave like this. Something calculated in the way she told her about the contract? Not straightaway. And how she went on with that gossip about Maximilian and Bella. As if to postpone telling her. Strange that she has never heard that. Good for Henry to be a new man. She said it but Sarah couldn't resist the jibe: 'You couldn't do it.' Perhaps not. But she admires people who can. Like that man in Malraux. The girlfriend sleeps with a colleague before a mission, a mission everyone knows he won't return from and when the woman tells the boyfriend, he reacts properly, like a new man, but inside he is consumed by old-fashioned feelings. Bourgeois jealousy, that's what it was, that's what she said, what was wrong with that? But Sarah screaming at her, in her own home, in her own kitchen. 'You don't really know yourself, you couldn't do it.' And that bloody bumblebee hitting the lamp, stupidly suicidal. At this time of the year, where had it come from? Must have been hatched in the house; that would be a nuisance. Might be others.

'They have to consider floating voters, don't they, Richard?' Colin says. Is he going to say anything? He can't only nod. Floating voters! People with no principles, no politics, seduced by cheap hand-outs, like some children accepting sweets. If it were up to her, floating voters would have their suffrage taken away, for good. None of her friends is a floating voter.

'Our partners are Swiss,' Charles says. 'I've come to like Zurich. If we win this competition then . . .' Yet another architectural project. He has taken a note pad from his back pocket. Last time he left a drawing on the table; what assured hands architects have. She kept it, still has it. An opera house somewhere in South America. Will he leave the drawing behind this time?

'How's the gallery?' Emilie asks Sarah.

Why is Sarah looking at her like that? At Emilie, who is smiling, at Emilie who's kind, who's sweet. Sarah must say something. Everyone is staring at her now.

'Well, you should ask Anna. She knows better than I do. She's in charge.' Her tone of voice. A scene, a scene from Sarah. Bloody unfair to ruin her party and to be so rude to Emilie. Emilie who's always interested in others.

'Anyone for a top-up? More bread?' No one wants anything. The silence. Would it be better if Sarah got up and left? She ought to be embarrassed. They're all friends, they can take it, but she is at someone's dinner table. No, no, she mustn't allow this. But what's there to do? Interrupted dinners are a bad omen. In novels, films, that's what they signify. The silence is eating everyone away.

How long can she go on making allowances? Tolerating this, her gloom, and not only today. Sarah needs a relationship, that's obvious. But how can anyone help her? Thirty years. Thirty years since they both stood in front of *Le déjeuner*. 'Ça vous plaît?' Which one said it? French for a few minutes. Exchanged addresses but didn't keep in touch, and then the shock and the pleasure, the feeling that they were old friends, that day, a few months later, the first week of term, running into each other at the Barber Institute. Three years, post-grads, inseparable.

'Now that I have your attention, let me tell you something,' Emilie says. Is she the saviour or is that it? 'I was at Tate Modern the other day, Anna's favourite building in London.' Her Juliette Binoche eyes smiling at her. She is sweet to remember, to say it.

'I was finishing my coffee, when a man sat down at my table and said he was sorry to be late. My first thought, obviously, was that he had mistaken me for someone else. Perhaps he was on a blind date, or something like that. But he seemed pleasant, interesting even, yes, yes, in that sort of un-English way—'

'Oh, là là, what does that mean?' Marc says. 'In the name of the *entente cordiale*, explain yourself.'

'Well, I don't know—'

'Oh Emilie, don't take him seriously,' Christina says. 'I know exactly what you mean.'

'So do I.' And she does. Of course she does. But she shouldn't have said that. She spoke in the name of female solidarity but Richard, Richard will remember it. 'Your Frenchman,' he will say. Must be thinking it now. How every word, every word that comes out spontaneously, that comes out sincerely, digs us in further. Zip up, Anna.

'Well, I don't know why, simply to be pleasant, perhaps, or curious, I said it was all right, I didn't mind waiting. He sat down and then I thought I ought to tell him that he had made a mistake. But before I could do that, he said he had brought the photos. And, I suppose it was a bit naughty of me, but I let him take them out of his bag. They were in a box, an old shoe box.'

Now, that's galvanised the table; even Sarah seems to be interested. And Richard's gloom has gone. 'He gave me the box and nudged me to open it. It was full, full of pictures, each sheet carrying sixteen small black and white photos, like those contact prints you sometimes get, the whole lot on one sheet. They were not very big, each two by one, centimetres, I mean. I peered closely. They were all of me. Can you imagine? But I had never met him before. What's more, he said they were taken during our holiday last year in a German spa resort. I wanted to tell him that it had all been a mistake, that it wasn't me, but I couldn't. The pictures clearly were of me. You could see us walking in a beautiful ornamental garden, or meeting in a terribly elegant hotel.'

'Did you recognise your clothes?' Christina asks.

'Yes, some of them. But the strangest thing was that I was wearing a necklace that Colin gave me for my birthday last year. You could see it clearly.'

'Wow. And you're telling us this? You spent some time with this bloke while Colin was busy writing?' Marc says.

'No, I didn't. We both know that since my birthday we haven't spent a day apart.'

'How strange,' Charles says. 'Photoshop? You can do anything. But why?'

'A stalker. He wanted to lure you—' Marc says.

'But I've never been to that place. I don't recall either the garden or the hotel.'

'Sometimes memory plays tricks with us.'

Emilie can't be this naïve. It's scary. She is beautiful; men notice her. Marc is right; it must have been a stalker. Had it been herself, she would have been scared. Gone to the police.

'So, what happened?'

'He gave me the box and left.'

'And that was all?'

'Yes. He left his mobile number.'

'They are lovely pictures. Beautiful actually,' Colin says.

'Somebody is playing a joke on you. Some prankster,' Charles says. 'I wouldn't take it seriously.'

'Stranger than fiction,' Richard says. At last he said something to the whole table, not only a few mumbled words to his neighbours. Emilie, wonderful Emilie. She has got them all talking, all focused on the same story. And what a story, but she shouldn't be taking it so lightly. There are weirdos around; they may look interesting but they can also be dangerous.

'Well,' Colin says as he and Emilie smile. What's happened to the tension? Even the two of them are in a better mood. 'Well,' Emilie says, 'the story I told you is the beginning of Colin's new novel—'

'My goodness, Emilie, you got us there,' Marc says. 'But you shouldn't have told us. It's like those stories where they tell you that it was all really a dream. A let-down, more likely. As a child, I was always disappointed when I came to the bit at the end where it says Alice woke up.' Complaining Marc. But others are smiling, even Richard, and Sarah. It will be all right, they will talk it through on Monday. If only she had not been so tense. She had no time to relax before dinner. Everything left to her, with him being late. All she could do was have a quick shower, letting the hot water run down her body, like a mountain stream washing away her worries – isn't that meant to help? She lay down for a few minutes and listened to Casals, trying to empty her head, but images of his spartan, chilly room kept crowding in. And all the time she was anxious that she would forget to put the CD

26

back in its hiding place under the jumpers. Richard would never go there, but if he did, he would be upset, hurt even, unfairly of course. Your Frenchman, he would say. It's so long ago, twenty-five years or more, well, has to be, twenty-seven, -eight even. They would fall asleep to cello music, curled up, Gustave's French words in her ears. Every now and then Richard hints at her 'love of the cello'. Once he even said 'lust for the cello' – was that deliberate or a slip of the tongue? But this is a digitally remastered version, the Casals recording. She heard it on the radio and had to buy it. She cares for the music. Nothing would convince Richard. A reminder, that's what he would think. 'You still love him.' Silly to be so insecure.

'So, what's the title of this one?' Charles says.

'Have a guess.' How could they? But they are trying. She won't have a go. Too much like a party game. How loud and excited they are, like children competing for a prize. No one guesses. Richard comes closest with his *Murder in Marienbad*. Of course – she should have thought of it – it's *The Last Day in Marienbad*, Colin tells them.

She will bring in the dessert. Marc is already collecting the plates. At least that stops him from lecturing everyone. Thank God he was late. His insistence on helping, when she has to juggle so many things, it makes life harder. And the mess he creates. Would his presence have deflected the tension between the other two?

She must follow him to the kitchen and take charge of the plates, otherwise he'll drop stuff on the floor. And they will walk on crumbs. He's probably already rearranging the shelves in her kitchen. Taking control, that's what he likes. And why is Christina coming downstairs?

'Been checking the babysitter's okay.'

'And?'

'Oh yes. Fine. But you never know with Jack.' How lucky she has been not to have given birth to a disabled child. How could you keep the house clean? No wonder Christina is so neurotic. She has had other worries with hers, everyone does. It never stops with children. But she is trying to let them go. She has stopped ringing them every day.

Marc is standing by the sink, staring into the dark. The plates are spread all over the worktop. Why couldn't he stack them up? Richard would have. Marc has had no house-training, no woman around. He smiles at her; he doesn't look as if he wants to return to the dining room.

'Did you like the dinner?'

'Marvellous. I always eat so well here. How do you have time to do it all? Anna, you're a wonderful woman. You can do everything.'

'Gosh, no. But it's good to hear you say that. Tell me. How are you?' He must know she means it. That's why she is asking him here, not in front of the others.' He sighs. 'It's that bad?'

'Yeees.'

'Can I do anything?' He shrugs. 'I'd like to help. If I can.' Yes, she would. But she has no idea how. And she has no time. But she has to ask, she has to offer. 'Tell me. Truly, let me help you.'

'I dragged myself out today. Haven't left the house for more than two weeks. Most of the time I lie in bed, with the blinds down, unable to move. It's all black . . .'

'It might help if you worked on something. Start a new painting . . .'

'You don't understand. I don't see anything. All the colour

has gone. How can I paint without colour?' Paint black pictures. Different shades of black. But she wouldn't say that. She has to be kind. And the pudding, she must get the pudding out. 'The muse has deserted me. It's happened before. But never for so long and I know, I'm certain, this time she won't come back. There's nothing any more.'

'Oh, here you are. Hiding from us,' Christina says, coming to the kitchen. This irritating cheerfulness about her. So false. 'Can I help with anything? Take anything back?'

'No, thanks. I'm about to get the pudding out.' A relief. A saviour. But not for him. Can anyone save him?

'So how's the painting?' Marc asks.

'Oh, there isn't any. I spend all my time being a mother. Charles is away a lot or out until late, and I ferry them around, feed them, wash them, teach them.' This loud laugh. 'People keep telling me it won't be for ever. They'll grow and I'll have time for myself. It doesn't seem as though it will ever happen. Oli's only four and Frida's barely one. Another fifteen years. And as for Jack, he's three but he will still need me at thirty-three. Unless they find a cure. But that's, that's unlikely.' Why does she say that? Rooting for sympathy? And this nervous laughter doesn't help; it's disconcerting.

'Hm. Sounds bad,' Marc says. 'Truly bad.' Is he trying to hurt her?

'Oh no, I'm not complaining. I'd have probably made a crap painter anyway. But when we were at art school, I . . . and you, can't deny it, we had all these great plans. And what's happened? Why? Where has it all gone?'

'To shit. Gone to shit. But Anna, Anna is a success. Look at her lovely home, the gallery, her children.' Drop the sarcasm, Marc. She has to give him a look. 'Sorry.'

Christina's smiling, puzzled. 'Has something happened, I mean, between the two of you, something I'm not aware of?'

Her party may yet be a failure.

She has to get the plates out. They are willing to help. It should occupy them. Anything is better than this self-pitying drivel. Her friends. These two people who want to talk about their unhappiness, these two people who want to hurt because they hurt.

Sarah's staring ahead, silent. Stiff shoulders . . . a bad sign. Has she fallen out with Charles? His face is flushed; he has turned away from her. Oh well, it might do her good to get the cold shoulder from everyone. That percentage. Even if they could manage, it's the principle. At least she agrees with her about the new artist, her discovery.

She must find someone for Marc. And for Sarah. Then she would stop being irritable. Yes, yes, she took the afternoon off, but she will catch up and stay late on Monday and Tuesday at least. But to accuse her of playing Mrs Dalloway, bloody unfair. And her sneer at that. She is envious of her home life, of the atmosphere at her parties. She wanted to hurt her. How dare she insinuate she is only a stay-at-home hostess?

But who, who for the two of them? Does she know anyone? A woman, two women, or would Sarah prefer a man this time? She has done it before, she has tried matchmaking, a thankless task. It's her own happiness with Richard, yes, that's what gives her hope. That's what makes her want to help others.

Marc's cutting the cake and decorating plates with slices of passion fruit.

'Make each one different, a work of art.' And that nervous laughter of Christina's. Her art training put to practice now as she blobs each plate with raspberry coulis.

'A dusting of cocoa?' Charles picks up a tea spoon and a strainer.

'Yes, that's a job for you. The finishing touch. Only an architect will do.'

'Anna likes beautiful pictures. Don't you, darling? But let's not eat them,' Colin says. Laughing at her. Laughing at what she said when they came in. But she loves them. She loves them all. And Richard. Was it the marquise or the duchess who went out? Colin knows. He's the novelist. It's up to him to decide. Yes, she loves them all.

A Hair Clasp

WE WENT SWIMMING, my daughter and I. She was twenty and a good swimmer. I didn't need to keep an eye on her. I read on the beach while she went into the sea. From time to time, I lifted my eyes from my book and looked at her. She would smile and raise an arm, as if in greeting. Or perhaps she wanted to say, 'Look at me,' as children often do, seeking recognition even when they are past their childhood. The last time I saw her, the waves had grown and the choppy sea tossed her around playfully. One moment she was hidden under the foamy whiteness, another moment she was riding the crest of the waves, shimmering against the glistening surface of the water. I smiled and thought how much I loved her. This happy young woman. I wanted to shout how lovely she looked, but there was no point as my voice would have been lost in the crushing power of the sea. So I greeted her with my hand up in the air and went back to my reading. The next time I looked up, I couldn't see her. I saw other swimmers, a dozen of them, enjoying the waves. I wanted to see her smiling and communicating her pleasure to me so I climbed a bridge next to where they were swimming. I still couldn't spot her. A thought crossed my mind that she may have drowned. I have always been a worrier but sometimes your worst fears come true. I looked harder, I moved around the bridge but I still couldn't see her. My chest tightened with fear. Was this really happening? Then I noticed a beautiful hair clasp, an antique piece that someone must have left there or, more likely, lost. The piece was lying on top of a stone pillar that formed part of the banister of the bridge. Cupping it in the palm of my hand, I caressed the pearly section held by its silver frame. The intricacy of its craft and the smoothness of the object charmed me. As I turned it around, sunshine played hide and seek on its surface. I would have loved to have it but the find was too valuable not to report. But something told me that I had the right to keep it. I clutched it firmly and walked home alone. I will be careful never to lose it.

To Complete the Thought

In memory of Max Lab (1938–2016)

THE THOUGHT THAT I would never see this man again was a painful one, Jocelyn wrote in a letter to me, and while the music played, this thought grew inside me, Jocelyn continued, Laurie said, until my awareness of everything that was not associated with him had gone and I worried about the time passing and my opportunity to be in his presence again abruptly coming to an end. The chances of running into him in a city the size of London, unless we had mutual friends, lived in the same area or shared particular and very specific, if not rare interests, very rare interests, so rare that there would be only one group, or only one class in the whole city and we would have to frequent the same place, which was unlikely to have been the case because we would have already known each other, therefore, the chances of meeting him were slight, so negligently slight that they may not have existed at all. I could not count on such serendipity, and even if that were to happen, for no matter how minuscule a window of opportunity, how trifling a chance, one in a million, one in ten million, even a complete leap in the dark, it was still a chance, it was still a possibility, I was telling myself, it was a kind of possibility that would keep hope alive, a possibility that would allow me to go through a day, a week, even months, and I could manage to sustain it for years and persevere until something else happened, an encounter, an event that created room to go on, but even if I were to run into him, I would have to be prepared that he may not remember me and that he may take me for one of those frightening people who accost strangers in public places and claim previous acquaintance, one of those awful people who could not be shaken off. I had to accept, Jocelyn wrote, that never seeing him again, although the thought of that was painful, was the most realistic outcome of the situation. I sat in a pew next to him, for we were at a concert in a church, and while everyone around me was listening to the music, my whole body and mind were alert to his movements as he leaned forward to readjust his coat in thick brown Crombie, which he had casually and clumsily folded, in that way that men tend to do and sometimes women too when they either do not look after their clothes or do not wish to give the impression that they care about their appearance. This coat, which he had pushed onto the shelf in front of us, kept unfolding itself and gradually slipping down, like some flocculent beast, Jocelyn wrote, some flocculent beast that was being born again and again. It was this development, this birthing, this waking up of the creature that required the man's renewed attention, so that he had to bend forward, push the unruly garment back into sleep and make sure that it did not interfere with his listening to the music. This coat became an intercessor between the man and me, an intercessor that, as will become clear in a moment, an intercessor that I very much welcomed. I needed that coat and its jittery nature, that coat with its will of its own, that coat was my ally.

In the time between each readjustment of the position of the coat, in that time lasting more than five but less than ten minutes, the man's right hand reached across to the ledge in front of us where I had placed the evening's programme. He did not seem to have his own copy, an observation that I made after the first time he consulted the programme, an observation I made with delight, de-light in my heart, as it alleviated the darkness, and although, let me make this clear, although it was only a temporary delight, it brought a ray of light into the sadness that was preoccupying me. I made that observation with a sense of hope too for it struck me immediately that sharing a programme might present an opportunity for more than our silent, tactile communication. With each of those movements, whether leaning forward to calm the restless coat with the push of his arm or to reach for the programme with his hand, his body came into a brief and barely felt contact with mine, and as the two movements produced a sensation in my body, a sensation that was of necessity different when the man performed the former movement from the sensation when he performed the latter movement, since each time a different part of his arm came into contact with a different part of my body, and the pressure exerted varied, enough for me to grade it in fine terms, and with each of these movements I was aware that we had initiated an intimacy, an intimacy that lasted a moment or two, an intimacy that I wanted to continue, that I couldn't bear losing once the concert was over. I knew how elusive such moments are, and I knew how rare they are, and yet when they come to us, they are so soon over and the dark returns. But the nature of our communication did not allow me to surmise the nature of his feelings towards me or towards the possibility of our future meeting and despite trying to read the signs, by which I mean the array of signs that stood for him in my eyes, I had no idea of what was on his mind, Jocelyn wrote.

There was something about the man's face that attracted me to him, something that I could neither single out nor define, and despite the sadness at the thought that I may never see him again, my attraction for him was so powerful that it took over my body, creating a nervous state of alertness, the kind that mixes pain with excitement, the pain that is close to pleasure and, while unable to bear the painful thought that I would never see him again, I also felt alive, alive with a flutter in my chest, that flutter that I had been familiar with from the spring times of my youth, Jocelyn wrote. The man's facial features were irregular, and there was a distinct raggedness about his skin, the raggedness that reminded me of those faces that have deep-cut lines around the mouth, like the opening and closing bracket, only that this man did not have the deep cuts around his mouth, but maybe it was not only the skin, it was his hair too that styled itself to unkemptness, and I do mean that it styled *itself*, for I do not think this man was in the habit of styling his own hair, nor inviting anyone else to do so, but it was not only the skin and hair, not even the clothes that he was wearing, for they were ragged too, not in a tatty and worn way, instead they were ragged in a manner that suggested the casual sartorial attitude of their wearer. But it wasn't only the face and hair and his outfit, or even his slight figure, it was the overall demeanour of raggedness that contributed to the impression of his appearance, but then it wasn't only the appearance, it was more the air about him, that attracted me. There was something about him that was compelling, compelling to me, for I would not claim that anyone else would have found him compelling. In fact, it is possible that it was precisely because I could not define my attraction for him, or at least part of that attraction, a major part, which created an air of mystery about him, of something unknown, of something hidden, that I found so appealing. The attraction I felt for him, or for something about him that I could not define, was as special as those rare instants when I come upon a word that visibly gratifies me, such as palimpsest used to, but these days such instants and such words are rare, Laurie, and when they do happen, they partly make up for enduring years of daily vulgarity.

The man glanced in my direction a few times, half smiling in the pleasant but conspicuously conventional way that English people have, the way that is both friendly and reserved at the same time and, to me at least, friendly and reserved in equal measure. And that was the problem, Jocelyn wrote, Laurie said. That has often been the problem and I can envisage that it will continue to be a problem. I am familiar with that look but I find it hard to judge which of the two aspects, friendly or reserved, dominates at particular times or with particular individuals. To me they appear of the same intensity but that must be because of my inability to read their appearance, for why would anyone wish to send such a confusing message? Unless, unless there is something perverse about their state of mind – a possibility that cannot be discounted – but how can I tell when that is the case? But if we can assume, of course assuming anything is a big if, if we can assume that a person does not deliberately set out to confuse, then we can say that someone smiling in a reserved sort of way must have decided beforehand what it is they wish to project to their collocutor. There is another difficulty here that we must take into account and that is the question of the execution of that decision, of that smile or of that holding-back grimace. When the sender is not fully versed in the art of smiling or does not have a knack for projecting reserve and therefore they have no proper control over the execution of their intention, over their decision that either the smile or the reserve should prevail, this difficulty, this lack of skill presents yet another complication. Since I do not wish to be unreasonable, and since I like to think of myself as a person who is happy to give everyone a second chance, and if not everyone, maybe not to two or three persons, that is, almost everyone, I am fully prepared to countenance that possibility because anything else might appear too intolerant on my part or give the impression that I was suggesting they are deliberately teasing, or even purposefully titillating my attention, only to slam it back into my face. As you can see, I do take these issues seriously, Jocelyn wrote, Laurie said, but I have to since it happens to me fairly often, maybe once a week, and I imagine one would consider that fairly often, it happens to me that a stranger, male or female, talks to me on the train or in a gallery, or in a supermarket, and they talk to me about something that may be considered private, such as their marital status, or extra-marital history, or their preference for a particular dish, sometimes they give details of an illness or refer to incest in their family, and they do it in what to me appears a casual, not-caring-whether-you-know-or-not manner, and then a person sets aside what her uncle did to her as if she'd never said it, as if I'd never heard it, and returns to questioning me if I didn't mind as to whether garlic in ratatouille should be chopped or put through a press. Such disclosures can be baffling and someone like me can find themselves in situations, not of their own making, that can become embarrassing, if not upsetting. For someone like me, who is foreign, and this is not simply a matter of nationality, of living in a country where I was not born, for

TEMPTATION: A USER'S GUIDE

someone like me is foreign in any place, even in the place where I was born and brought up. From what I know of other people, I would say that they would define someone as not a foreigner if they satisfied these two conditions, that is, they couldn't be a foreigner in a place where they were born and brought up. But for me, being foreign has nothing to do with these so called conditions, being foreign does not depend on physical displacement, being foreign is a matter of not sharing the views of others, of the majority, being foreign means not taking for granted their values, not understanding to the point of not being able to guess the reactions and the social mores of those around me, whom we could call the natives, being foreign is not believing that there is such a thing as common sense, being foreign is about not believing that there is such a thing as human nature – that ubiquitous concept people use so frequently when they wish to justify their own views, or give credence to their own values, when they want to justify themselves, but to someone like me that concept is completely nonsensical – and when put like this, one can see that a native is anyone whose views are the views of the rest of the group, regardless of whether they were born and brought up in the same place as other members of the group and therefore being foreign is more a matter of temperament rather than of birth and passport. As a comedy character might say, sometimes one is born a foreigner, in other cases one has the status of a foreigner thrust upon one. When one is born a foreigner, that is a case of temperament, a case of some kind of indefinable disposition, and sometimes one becomes a foreigner, either because one has moved away from a country of their birth, a case of a physical exile, or because one's upbringing, one's environment has made one think and behave in particular ways, which is a case of a mental exile. It is what our culture, so dependent on binary oppositions, Laurie, calls the case of either nature or nurture, Jocelyn wrote. With some people, and that has been my situation, the two, the physical and the mental exile have converged, with the mental exile preceding and possibly bringing about the physical exile. But these situations are not static and fixed, indeed, there is a cultural expectation on a foreigner to evolve into a native, or a partial native at least. The status of a foreigner, and it is a status, low or high in our social hierarchy, depending on one's ideological make up, this status has a shelf life and after you have lived in a country for a certain number of years, say more than five or ten, your privileges, the excuses that the natives would accept for your confusion, for your faux pas, for your passivity or for your forwardness, for your inability to understand the notion of common sense, all of that expires and you are expected to take on some of the mores of the natives. No mitigating circumstances, such as the defendant saying but I am a mental exile, I have been like this even amongst the people where I was born, none of that is taken into account. Someone like me, who has lived in a country that is not the country of their birth for years, has to know how to respond in social situations with the natives. As you can imagine, the situation works the other way, too: as much as a foreigner does not know how to read the natives, the natives do not know how to judge the foreigner. If he speaks their language with less than a native competency, they tend to think of him as being of a simple mental capacity, a juvenile, not a full citizen. The judgement of the natives adds new elements to the collage of the foreigner's self-identity and when the foreigner looks in the mirror they see someone different from what they expected, they appear to themselves different from what they thought they were. That is at the heart of being foreign: you see yourself as different from what you thought you were. Dear Laurie, Jocelyn wrote, it is very important that you are familiar with these ideas if you wish to understand the situation at that concert.

To complete the thought, Laurie, Jocelyn wrote, I didn't know how to read the face of that man, his smile and his glances. Each time I saw him glancing at me – for it is my belief that he was glancing at me – I wondered whether he wanted to say something to me, whether he was interested to know what I thought of the music, whether, I wondered, he might want to know anything about me or even whether he might have experienced the pain at the thought of not seeing me again, the pain similar to the one I felt at the thought of not seeing him again. At the same time, I was wondering why, if that had been true, why hadn't he then spoken to me. I tried to help him, that is, assuming that he wanted to be helped, and to that end, I moved the programme, my copy of the programme, I slid it along the stand towards him so that the sheet lay equidistantly positioned from me as it did from him. This was my way of telling him, this was my way of making clear how I felt about our communication, but my movement wasn't entirely selfless since the resulting placement of the programme made me feel as if we had an object that we shared, a feeling that we were together in some way, Jocelyn wrote, it was an object that was binding us together, no matter how tenuous that bond was. But there was something else too that made me wonder why he hadn't initiated anything beyond those movements to attend to his coat or to look at the programme, and use the opportunity to glance at me, that is, unless you wish me to consider those movements as part of his intentions towards me, and I am not saying that I was discounting those movements, for it is perfectly possible to see those movements as a way of his initiating contact. I was thinking that since he was a man in his late sixties and while I am not suggesting that he should have known what he wanted to do, or that he should not have been shy because the idea that one knows oneself, or that one becomes less shy as one ages, or indeed that one becomes more mature, is not the one I subscribe to. In an ideal world, yes, *nosce te ipsum*, know thyself, is a commendable maxim, but that is not how it works in life, at least not with me or with those I know. But when I say that he was in his late sixties, I mean that age too, similar to the foreignness, carries certain privileges, the privileges that remain, in fact, unlike those of foreignness, which wear off gradually, the privileges of age increase as time passes. Age brings about certain allowances and therefore if he wanted to say something to me, if he genuinely was interested in establishing contact, if the thought of not seeing me again was painful to him, or if not painful, if the thought of not seeing me was not something he was happy with, even if the thought of not seeing me again was something that he wasn't entirely indifferent to, he would have been able to do something about it and his age would have absolved him of any potential embarrassment. Of course, Laurie, you will know that I was aware that this was my thinking, this was what I would have felt had I been in my late sixties and had I been at a concert in a church sitting next to someone I wanted to but didn't dare address. The idea of age as a privilege, as a licence to speak and act your mind, was my own and I, with my foreignness, my foreignness that was no longer acceptable, my foreignness that should no longer have been tolerated, or not wholly tolerated, I with my foreignness that existed nevertheless, I was the last person who should have assumed that others might share my views let alone that my attitudes were the normative ones. I had no idea whether he wanted to speak to me, Jocelyn wrote, whether the thought of not seeing me again was painful to him, or whether it was making him unhappy, just as I had no answers as to why he didn't do anything, why he didn't say anything to me. For someone like me who is a foreigner, for someone like me who is at a loss how to read the signs of the world around, someone like me could not tell whether his movements to adjust his coat – for it was a scruffy garment and he could have easily let it fall on the ground – meant that he was giving attention to the coat or to me. If I can remind you, we have a friend whose clothes are even scruffier than the clothes worn by the man sitting next to me; they are so scruffy that once this friend of ours was walking down Knightsbridge and stopped to check a menu posted outside one of the restaurants, when an elderly man pushed a tenner into his hand and before this friend of ours, who is a university professor of some standing and by no means someone who needs a tenner not to hunger, before he could work out what has happened, his benefactor rushed away. I hear you say, now, this may have been a one-off occurrence, Laurie, Jocelyn wrote, and you could be right but I have no way of agreeing or disagreeing with you since our particular friend, who is a professor, a scientist of some eminence, is no longer in contact with us. But my point is that the professor, our friend, who is so scruffy that those who do not know him take him for a beggar, this friend, has the habit of folding his clothes and meticulously storing them. You wouldn't see him hanging his overcoat on a peg, would you, oh no, nothing but a good padded hanger would do. Knowing that, I was careful not to draw any conclusions about the man sitting next to me and to think that because his clothes were scruffy, his constant tidying up of his coat, no matter how clumsy, was a sign to me, an expression of his desire that his body should touch mine. And then I noticed that the coat that had previously appeared to be a small, helpless bundle requiring care not to fall onto the floor, the care which brought about physical contact between my shoulder and the man's upper arm, and was therefore welcome, at least on my part, this coat now reminded me of a rootless person in an oversized winter garment, no longer unfolding itself slowly, instead, this home-less creature who had been asleep and was now waking up and raising their head, with their initial air of disorientation giving way to discontent, the discontent that was loud in the way that heavy cloth can be when it rubs against itself. The spectacle of the jerky movements of the creature was now forcing the man, this man with an intriguing face sitting next to me, to attend to their demands, and so he leaned forward and tried to calm down the homeless creature by laying both hands on it, faith-healer fashion. He was leaning forward in a straight line, instead of sideways as before, and that gesture, unlike the previous one, meant that his body no longer came into contact with mine. The coat, the intercessor between the man and me, our pander, my ally, my friend, the coat, with its demands on the man with an intriguing face, had turned my foe, it had turned interloper, Jocelyn wrote, an interloper commanding the man's attention to the extent that I couldn't expect that there would be any left for me.

As for the programme, each time the man leaned forward

and reached for it, I had no way of knowing whether it was the programme or me he wanted to consult. Being of a perennially optimistic nature, a tiny bit kept hoping that the man's constant need to look at the programme and check the order in which the music was being played, when there were only seven pieces by three composers altogether – for most people, whether they were regular concert goers, music lovers or not, an occasional glance, no more frequently than when one piece finished and another one started, would have been enough – meant that his interest in the programme was a way of creating opportunities to establish communication with me. At the same time, I was thinking of what might happen if I was misreading his glances and he had no intention or desire to communicate with me, for it sometimes happens and to someone like me more often than to you, Laurie, or to others, that I read the actions of people around me differently from the way they intend them to be read, and sometimes the difference between my reading of the action of another person and the intention of the other person is diagonally opposite and, remembering that at the concert, I could not help thinking that the man with the intriguing face could have been looking at me not because he wanted to initiate communication but as a way of warding off any approach from me. Or, he could have been one of those people who are friendly even to the point of starting a conversation, but then walking away or withdrawing by giving you one of those looks that tell that you have overstepped the boundaries of civilised communication, that you have gone too far in your inquisitiveness, that you have thrown caution to the wind with your assumed familiarity, that you have committed an indiscretion and that nothing can follow after that for you will be cut off, ostracised in the eyes of the other, and in the more extreme cases, told off, reprimanded, possibly even loudly and in public, strongly enough for everyone to see and hear. The man with an intriguing face, casting glances in my direction, for so I thought, he could have been encouraging me, even tempting me to start a conversation, only to spurn my efforts, turn away from me or have a laugh at my expense. Those were some of the possibilities that might have acted themselves out and sitting there, so close to him, and yet despite such proximity having no idea of his thoughts, I had no way of knowing which course the events would take. When I have found myself in similar situations in the past – for yes, you know, Laurie, I have been in situations in theatres, in cinemas, and even more commonly at lectures and literary readings, where a person on my right or my left, or sometimes even both of them, elicited my interest to the point where all I could think was to imagine what they were like and how I could go about finding that out – in such situations, I had difficulties focusing, or fully focusing on seeing or hearing whatever activity it was that we had gathered to see or hear and all my mental efforts were focused on the person or persons in my vicinity but never to the extent I experienced this time. But even if I could compare the extent to which I lacked concentration in those past situations with this one at the concert and even if I had come to the conclusion that the lack of focus this time was more or less equivalent to the situations in the past, the difference this time was the pain. In all those previous situations, the dominant, if not the only impulse, was the desire to initiate a verbal exchange, purely out of inquisitiveness, I believe, but this time I knew that the verbal exchange, if I could establish it, would only be the way leading to another meeting. For it was the thought that I may never see this man again that was so painful to me, as you know, Jocelyn wrote, Laurie said.

My feelings of pain may sound surprising coming from someone like me, someone who is so different from other people, someone who enjoys solitude, a person who does not crave the company of others, and saying this ('person who does not crave the company of others'), I am being kind to myself, as you, Laurie, will know, and so you might accuse me of misrepresenting myself but it would be more true to say that I am someone who more often than not has misanthropic thoughts and these thoughts are usually provoked by what I can only refer to as the increasingly frequent displays of vulgarity on the part of the general horde – or shall I say herd – of those who have in the years since my youth taken to eating on trains, and not only on trains, in most public places, and I don't mean having the occasional pretzel or an ice cream when in a holiday mood, but I am talking of individuals of all ages eating fried food and licking their greasy fingers, or even sucking noodles from a pot while riding on the tube. And don't start me on . . . suffice it to say that there is no end to activities that feed my dislike and fear of, Jocelyn wrote, and fear of, Jocelyn wrote again, said Laurie, of humankind.

To be abrupt, to complete the thought, the experience of similar situations in the past was telling me that I had no reason to fear rejection or embarrassment unless I initiated a move towards the man in the pew next to me and that meant that as long as I didn't do anything, I had nothing to fear from him. At the same time, the thought, the thought that once the concert was over, in an hour or so, I was unlikely to see the man again unless I did something, that thought that I would never see him again was such a one that the choice of not doing anything and letting things take their painful course was not an option I could accept. Things taking their painful course would have meant that at the end of the concert, after the applause and after the bows and after the encores, one or two encores, for three is very rare indeed, I can hardly remember a concert with three encores and since three encores are so rare I am sure I would remember it, so I was thinking that after one or two encores, if no communication were established, the man with the intriguing face and I would take our separate paths. I cannot say that we would have parted because, as you, Laurie, can see, we had never been brought together, and yet all those movements to tidy up his coat, obsessively repetitive and his – shall I call it addictive? – need to return to the programme – for there was not much to read, I am talking of one A5 sheet of paper with the titles of seven musical pieces on it – and therefore create opportunities for corporeal contact between our two selves, the contact, no matter how momentary and slight, was not to be spurned and it was this contact that had made me feel that although nothing was said, he, this man with an intriguing face, and I had established a kind of unspoken intimacy, a kind of relationship that had to carry on. But that was unlikely to be the case and the thought was so painful and becoming more painful with each note which the musicians played, that I knew I had to do something regardless of the consequences. I did not need to remind myself, as I sometimes have to, although not often, I did not have to tell myself that I must allow nothing to deter me from my aim. But even as I have more or less come to the conclusion to act, I knew that I had made no progress because the real decision, and it was not so much a decision, for not acting was not an option since its consequences were much too painful, but the real issue was a choice, the real question was to choose what to do. I had to think of something that would allow me to speak to him without it appearing as if I was dragging him into a conversation that he, possibly, or most likely – I had to make that assumption – didn't want to be in. I had to think of something that would make our exchange appear casual and non-threatening, something that would disguise my eagerness to see him again – oh, the impossibility – and therefore could be stopped without a big scene of rejection that would show me up, or make me the centre of a public display. But of the three outcomes that I mention here, I must say that the first one is the only one that I feared and while the others would by their nature mean rejection too, the fact that he might have reacted loudly and ostentatiously, drawing attention to me approaching him, would not have bothered me because someone like me, someone who is used to being different, someone who has unfailingly been a foreign element, does not pay much attention to what others think. But the fact is that whether he chose a public rejection or a quiet one, and by quiet I could envisage him returning a piece of paper to me after, let's imagine, Jocelyn wrote, I have slipped him one saying in a few words, very few indeed, that I wanted to see him again and enclosing my telephone number or an e-mail address. But that rejection would not even have to come straightaway, while we were at the concert and the music was still playing and there was a chance of one or two encores, no, that rejection could have been spread over days or weeks, even months while I was waiting for him to get in touch. I could see myself leaving the concert, having given him my number or my e-mail address, full of hope and expectation and then checking my messages as soon as I reached home, or making sure that my phone was still working or the landline was not cut off, or the receiver was not off the hook and then spending the next week, or weeks, waiting to hear from him and then gradually realising when nothing happened that he was rejecting me, that he was spurning my move, that he had no interest in me and telling myself that I was wasting my life on waiting and when that became difficult to take, trying to persuade myself, and that might happen in time to come anyway, trying to persuade myself that he had never existed and that his intriguing face, whose attraction I felt but could not describe, that that face was once again, as you sometimes say in your letters, and which I have to rebut as a stereotype, a too simplistic stereotype, that he was a projection of my desire, of something that I have been aware of missing in myself and have been looking for in others. Oh, how clearly I could see it all happening, Jocelyn wrote, and I could feel his sigh, Laurie said. Because of all these possible developments that might follow my passing him a slip of paper with my address or phone number, that course of action, I mean the piece of paper with a note on it, was not the option I could choose. The only way was to speak to him directly, to say exactly what was on my mind and cut out those days, weeks or months of waiting. Get it over and done with. Face the situation. Look at it squarely. *Courage, mon frère, mon semblable.* You are a man with an intriguing face and I cannot bear the thought that I would never see you again. I was also thinking that it would be more honest to come clean completely and say that the thought of never seeing him again was too painful to bear. But would it have been? Perhaps, but that could be construed as emotional blackmail, the thought of which I would find unacceptable and would employ on no account, not because I have moral scruples about blackmail per se but because the situation I was in and the way I was thinking about my options, weighing the pros and contras, was entirely and hundred per cent rational and I would have felt very uncomfortable with introducing emotions. That is why I found the possibility that my words to him, honest and transparent as they were meant to be, could have been construed as emotional blackmail so objectionable that I preferred not to come clean and use the former rather than the latter option. The idea of talking to him, that decision, for I have gradually come to the decision that I had to speak to him, that idea came to me as the second section of the programme, which was Bach, gave way to the third and the last one. Vivaldi. I do not think that was a coincidence for I have never been a Vivaldi fan and had no great expectations for the final section of the programme and as it often happens when we do not have high expectations, we are pleasantly surprised and I must say that despite my concentration on how to act in the situation I found myself in, the music did have the effect on me in the same way as a trusted friend might have done at the time, someone who understood me and who could clearly see the situation and the dilemma I was faced with and who, carefully judging all of that, gave me a go-ahead, a warm and supportive encouragement with a light touch on the shoulder and a few softly spoken words. Yes, Vivaldi's music, as soon as the first few bars reached my ears, that combination of modal counterpoint with tonal logic of cadences, and the fact that I was aware of it, let alone its effect, that in itself was a minor miracle and I mean minor, Jocelyn wrote, for it is understandable that in a situation of some distress, in a situation of pain, it is a sympathetic intervention that we react to and hence I can understand that while I had hardly heard the music from the previous sections and in my memory all the notes, all the bars blurred into one, when Vivaldi came, my ears opened up and I listened. Oh Vivaldi, the magic of Vivaldi, you may say but there is a good scientific explanation for what was happening to me. I am thinking of the uses of the music of Vivaldi in treating people with dyslexia, with behaviour problems, with the inability to get to the point, as practised by that famous French otolaryngologist, with Gérard Depardieu as one of his patients. Therefore I wasn't surprised that Vivaldi lifted something in me, freed me from a veil of confusion, Jocelyn wrote, that was preventing me from seeing the situation more clearly: for a brief moment at least I knew, I was convinced, I was as sure as ever, that I had to act. And that was a good thing, undoubtedly a good thing.

In fact, while Vivaldi played I could see that the man with the intriguing face, the man sitting next to me, was going through the same thoughts as I was, wondering how he should approach me and fearing that I might freeze him out, or tell him that he had gone too far, that I was not interested in him and that it was preposterous to bother people at a concert when they have come to listen to music. The man with the intriguing face sitting next to me was having the same unbearable thought that once the music was over and the applause and the two encores had been played, most likely two for three is so rare that one could not count on that possibility, that man was fearing that after two encores he would never see me again. That man with the intriguing face sitting next to me, that man feared embarrassment and rejection, possibly as much as me, and possibly even more and who could say that his fears were not of at least the same magnitude as mine? But then another thought struck me, one of those ideas that when it comes, you start kicking yourself for not realising it before, one of those ideas that makes everything fall into place. The man was a foreigner. His intriguing face, by which I meant the face that I could not define, a face that was different from all other faces that I have ever seen, and yet it was a face that was familiar, a face that I remembered, it was a foreign face. As a foreigner, I thought, he was a man free from blind participation in the rituals of the natives, free from their customs, free from their moral codes. As a foreigner, he would not be a foreigner to me – isn't that right, Laurie? Jocelyn wrote. A foreigner to natives is not a foreigner to another foreigner – and that would mean that he, the man with the intriguing face, he would welcome my overture, no matter how unacceptable it were to the natives, that is, as a foreigner, he would read my signs in the same way that I have intended them. 'I, the man with an intriguing face, I want to speak to you,' I heard him say. I nodded. I will. I will. I will speak to you. I will speak to you. And as Vivaldi played, and the third section of the programme was longer than the previous two, I began to wonder how I could reassure the man with the intriguing face that he had nothing to fear and that my view of concerts, and my view of theatre performances and my view of public lectures and my view of literary readings and, up to a point, my view of visits to galleries and museums, was that they were occasions where we didn't go to listen to music or see a play, experience a work of art, think of ideas and arguments presented by a lecturer, my view was that these were opportunities to meet someone, someone who has gone there with exactly the same thought as us, meaning to meet someone like us. That is what everyone does, that is what everyone thinks, that is what everyone hopes, but no one, no one to my knowledge, has ever admitted it. It had to take two foreigners, Jocelyn wrote, and he underlined two foreigners, Laurie said, it had to take two foreigners to realise what theatres and concerts and exhibitions are all about. Suddenly I saw it all as clearly as written out in a book. At that point I remembered our other friend who used to tell us that when he went to the theatre, which he did as often as once a week, only one person sat next to him and the seat on the other side was regularly left empty, not to mention that there had been occasions, by no means rare, when the seats on both sides were left unoccupied and that, he told us, would not have been worth mentioning if the performance had been poorly attended but he was talking of the shows that were sold out and where he could not see, no matter how hard he tried, any other empty places in the whole of the auditorium. At that point, he would start describing the interior of the theatre and the seating arrangements, I like to be accommodating but his obsession with detail – something he assured me, he insisted to me, he had inherited from his grandmother – might have tested another person's patience, but someone like me understands that it is not given to every life to be a précis. But that aside, I had my doubts about what he was saying and without going into the reasons for those doubts right now, let me only mention that my feeling was that he was exaggerating, and again, I do not wish to explain now as it would mean going off on a tangent and it is a good idea to stick to the point, but I am sure it would have occurred to anyone, as it did to you, Laurie, that our friend's behaviour might have been prompted by his desire to call attention to himself and that all his talk about others avoiding to be in his proximity was nothing but a cry, a cry for sympathy. I am afraid, I must disagree with that. For now, let me simply say that I had my doubts about our friend's claim and, wishing to give him a fair hearing, I joined him a few times and I can testify that on each occasion the seat on his right – I was on his left – remained unoccupied and whenever I sat on his right, the seat on his left stayed vacant. Had it happened once or twice or thrice even, I would have attributed this empty seat next to him to a coincidence, but since it happened each time over the period of the six months that I was either with him, or, on those occasions when I was not, I rang him and checked with him immediately after the event, as soon as he reached home, in order to be able to make a note of the state of affairs and make sure that he was not exaggerating, I could see that the situation was deliberately engineered. But who was behind it? Was it himself, a deliberate deviousness in him to fool people into thinking no one wanted to sit beside him. But our friend is not devious. We know our friend in total. We can vouch for him. Who was orchestrating this unfortunate, unfortunate for him, series of situations? And why would they be doing it? Our friend was a pleasant man, kept himself to himself, had no trace of halitosis. It occurred to me that his name could have been placed on a blacklist of people who have a history of being a nuisance to be sat next to, of people who have a tendency to approach strangers occupying places on their left or right, or both. If that had been the case, it would have been entirely unjustified for his name to be on such a list for as I say and as we know our friend, Laurie, but without knowing whether he was on it, he had no chance to protest to the compilers and ask them to amend their mistake. I did suggest to him that since under the Data Protection Act he had every right to check whether indeed his name was on such a list, that he should do so even if it was not only a matter of writing a letter but involved a small fee, a fee that I would think in his case would have been well spent. I have not heard from him recently – have you? – and I am not privy as to whether he followed my advice or not. Leaving aside that question as to whether he had contacted them or not, or in case he did, the question of how the matter was resolved, it seemed to me that the only way out for him was to visit those theatres where seats are not numbered and he could then choose a place in between the two people already seated. That was the way, a clear solution to how he could beat the system that so unfairly deprived him of social opportunities available to most people in theatres.

Let me not lose the thread, Laurie, Jocelyn wrote, Laurie said. Once the last notes of Vivaldi were over, the applause brought on an encore and the next round of applause led to the second encore, none of which was Vivaldi, and that may explain what happened next. Without turning my head to the left, where the man with the intriguing, attractive face was sitting, I glanced at him and the thought that I will never see this man again became even more painful than before, which was understandable for I had spent two hours in his presence, two hours of wonderful intimacy, two hours that were coming to an end and there was nothing beyond that end. Nothing. The inevitability of us going our separate ways was too much to bear and I was assailed by the sense of loss for the intimacy that I had just experienced. I knew that the situation I was in would never be repeated and that he was for ever lost to me and I knew I had to act for my time was running out and then my time did run out, and there was no more choice whether to make a jump or not, that jump that up till then I feared could have destroyed that intimacy that we, or I, have had. It was that sense of loss that came to me as sadness that was telling me that I had to act since there was nothing else to do and as I cast my glance in his direction I could tell, there was no ambiguity this time, I could tell for sure that he too was telling me to do something, to act, I could hear his voice saying, 'Speak to me, you, the person sitting next to me,' and that voice now was much louder and much clearer than before and my awareness of the need to follow his encouragement produced a sense of weariness that took hold of me in a way that was paralysing, so utterly paralysing, or not quite paralysing, partially so, Jocelyn wrote, Laurie said, to me.

Baking For Love

THE CAKE-BAKER

Each morning she awoke and baked a cake.
It gave, she said, a meaning to her days.
The cakes she baked she stored in air-tight tins.
When all the tins were filled she took the cakes
and fed them crumbled to the ducks and drakes.
Then baked more cakes to store in air-tight tins.
Cakes none but undiscerning ducks would taste.

SACHA RABINOVITCH

SOMETIMES, AND THERE are days when it happens often, she said, sometimes, she needs to stop thinking about being a failure, sometimes, she wishes to escape from such thoughts, and while that is not entirely possible, while she cannot stop thinking about being a failure completely, she can make an effort to reduce the intensity of her thoughts about being a failure and she can make an effort to have a little respite from thinking that she is a failure and when she wants to do that, she needs to focus on a task, on a task that is very different from her main preoccupation, that of thinking and that of writing, on a task that makes her work with her hands and allows her thoughts to wander freely in a field of wild flowers that is not really a field of wild flowers but that is what it feels like for her thoughts as they freely move, like butterflies fluttering from one swaying poppy to another, and when she thinks of her thoughts freely moving she sees a field of white flowers in the sunshine. There are no occupations she engages in that allow her to work with her hands and to have her thoughts wander freely, there are very few occupations she can engage in that satisfy both conditions, in fact there is hardly anything that helps her not to think that she is a failure, and even then not thinking about being a failure is only temporary, a little respite only, and that one thing, that one occupation that helps is baking cakes. So she bakes, she bakes a cake, or two cakes, sometimes three, and she bakes scones and puddings, and she makes tarts and then there are days when there are quite a few cakes, quite a few puddings, quite a few tarts, quite a few scones sitting on her kitchen worktops, she said, more than she could possibly eat, even if she were to eat only cakes, or only scones, or only puddings, or only tarts, too many baked things for one person. And on such days she thinks, she said, that baking a cake is pure pleasure but having a cake baked is not so pleasurable because it has to be eaten, it cannot be just looked at, and she always has too many cakes, too many puddings, too many tarts, too many scones for one person.

With all this baking, it is no wonder that she has become good at baking and the other day, someone, someone who sometimes tastes her cakes, that someone said that she should be baking to live and not living to bake, and when she did not understand his words because she was living to bake and baking to live and she wondered what the difference was and he said he meant that she should be making her living with baking. She knew that was not possible because baking was too important to her and when something is as important as baking is to her, you cannot turn it into a commercial activity but some people only think of cashing in on everything and for her that was not possible, it certainly was not possible with baking because if she had to bake to sell she could not bake, she would get bored and even before she became bored all the cakes would fall apart or turn into crumbs as there would be nothing to hold them together if she were baking to sell. And that someone who said she should be baking to live – or was it the other way round? – she cannot remember, that someone who actually said that she should be baking to sell, as if baking to sell and baking to live were the same things, that someone also said that she should not be baking to get it over with, only he did not use such words, for they are her words and people do not use such words, even people she knows, even people who would say they are her friends, except perhaps one or two of them use such words. And he was not the first person to say that she could bake for a living, that is how good she was, yes, others have said that over the years but they don't understand that that is not what baking is about for her. She needs to bake in the same way that some people need to go for a walk, for a spot of fresh air, like some people need to have a drink, or a puff, or a spliff, but she has never said that to anyone because even she did not understand why she was baking. The other day she heard someone say that baking a cake was about love, that baking a cake was about giving love and she almost laughed for how could it be about love if you had no one to whom you could offer a slice, let alone a whole cake, she said. When her children were younger, when they were still children, she was a Jewish mother, she was a cliché of a Jewish mother, her children said. She was a Jewish mother without being Jewish, because she was always baking, always offering cakes and then, in those days when her children were children, baking was about love, about giving love. But those days when her children were children are gone and she is not a Jewish mother any more, she is not a cliché Jewish mother feeding her children and so there is no one to eat her cakes, no one who would say to her more than those ducks she sometimes feeds her cakes to, no one she could watch eat her cakes, eat them with pleasure, with gusto, smacking their lips as they bite into her cake and that would give her pleasure, as it used to once, but that feeding, that feeding with love, that is no more and so baking cakes is no more about love. Those days are gone and for her baking cakes is about not having love, not getting love, not giving love. But don't get me wrong, she said, she does not wish for those days to come back but if there were someone she could bake a cake for, if there were such a someone, she would bake it with love and when they ate it, perhaps they could feel the love she had put into it and perhaps she would get their love too. But why would she do that, why would she put love into a cake for someone, for someone she does not love? No, she does not mean this last bit, that last bit about putting love in a cake, she said, she most certainly does not mean that, she said, for the fact is that sometimes she gets all sentimental and thinks of the days when she was a Jewish mother and she liked being a Jewish mother because that is what her children used to call her because her children said in those days when they were still children, they said that she had taught them the importance of education, the importance of improving themselves and she had fed them, she had always offered them food, cakes and biscuits, breads and rolls, stews and bakes, she cooked and taught them and that was love, cooking and teaching her children. But baking for just anyone or baking for no one, as is her case now, that is not about love, that is not special or not very special, although it could be just a bit special, as with that woman, that woman she did not know very well but has met a few times, the woman who had tasted her cakes because she knocked on her door to ask something about parking regulations, or something like that, because she did not know what they were but perhaps that was just an excuse to knock on her door because no one would come in and ask for an explanation of parking regulations because everyone can read the signs on the pavement. But that woman said that she did not know the parking regulations because the woman said, I do not live in the street and I stay here only from time to time with a friend, a male friend, a gentleman friend, the woman said, and my friend lives down the road but he is not in now and so I cannot ask him but I need to wait for him and I do not know when he will be back and so I need to park and I need to park in this street, the adjoining streets will not do as I have lots of bags to deposit in his house because we are preparing to go on a trip round the world and we need to take lots of clothes with us and we need to take comforting items, the kind of comforting items one needs on a long trip, a trip around the world, such as my favourite bedside lamp – the light of hotel lamps is always too poor for night time reading or for making crochet – and I am taking my patchwork quilt too, the woman said. I could not be without my patchwork quilt for a long time, the woman said.

That woman had knocked on the door just as she was about to prick an apricot and almond brandy cake still in the oven and there was a chocolate sponge, freshly iced, and a lemon cake, already drizzled, cooling on a rack on the table and an apple pie, still in the tin next to the cooling rack and the woman made a comment, the woman said something but she could not remember what it was, perhaps something about the lovely smell and then the woman said have you just baked a cake, and she did not say anything to a question like that – because what could one say to a question like that? – and the woman smiled and the woman was looking at the cakes cooling on the rack and so she had to offer a taste, just a tiny taste of something, and she did not mind offering the woman a small piece of lemon cake, although the woman did not interest her and her lack of interest had nothing to do with the woman and more to do with her because in her days, she said, not many people interest her, in fact very few people interest her and, to be precise, hardly anyone interests her. The woman said something about the lemon cake being good, very good indeed, the woman said and the woman made one of those horrible noises of appreciation and immediately, while the woman was still masticating the last mouthful of the slice the woman had been offered, the woman glared at the chocolate sponge cake cooling on the rack on the table and the woman glared at the apple pie still in its tin and the woman made a comment, something about them looking good or yummy, yes, the woman used that infantile word, the word that rhymes with tummy, and a word she cannot stand and so it surprised her that she offered the woman a slice of the chocolate sponge and of the apple pie as well. Perhaps that was excessive but she felt, she said, that she had to offer the other two cakes to the woman to taste and that is not quite right because she is past the days when she felt that she had to do anything that other people expected her to do, she said, because that is the privilege of old age, the privilege that you can scupper conventions and you can be as eccentric as you want to, not that she thinks that offering a small slice of cake to a woman who wanted to know about parking regulations in her street was eccentric. Sometimes she wonders whether this rule – or is it a convention, or an expectation? – sometimes she wonders whether this expectation may be of her own making only, and so she wonders whether this privilege of old age to scupper conventions is true for everyone and whether other old people follow it but she has never asked anyone and so she cannot tell whether she alone has thought of this rule and appropriated it for herself but if the former were the case and the world allowed older people a certain amount of leeway to depart from social norms, then, she often wonders, would that be because society does not take old people seriously, or are there some other reasons, such as that old people have earned the right to do as they please, she said, earned the right to do as they please by kneeling down in corners of kitchens when they were children, misbehaved children, and facing blank walls, kneeling down and facing a lifetime of blank walls. That is something she will have to ponder on, she said, but, to get back to the woman in her kitchen that day, it so happened that the woman tried all three cakes on that occasion but not because she felt that she had to offer her to try the cakes after the woman had been glaring at them and smiling at them, and smiling at her, and commenting on the cakes, but something inexplicable happened and she who does not like other people or has not liked other people for some time now, felt that that woman was not too bad and that was the reason, that was the sole reason why she offered her the cakes. Nothing else was on her mind, nothing else at all, there was no thought of giving cakes and getting love from the woman, none at all, absolutely none, she is certain of that because she is past the days when she offered love and she is past the days when she wished for love from others.

And then there was a next time, oh yes, she said, there was a next time as the woman knocked again on her door and the woman said my friend, my gentleman friend is not in and I wonder if you would do me a favour and let me use your phone so that I could check when he would be back and so that I can collect my bags from him because our trip around the world has been postponed – only for a month but still postponed – and I need to get back my patchwork quilt and my favourite bedside lamp and my clothes and my shoes. So the woman came in and again there were cakes in the kitchen, as there often are, freshly baked cakes and there were scones too, a dozen or so herb scones and half a dozen sweet ones and again the woman made a comment on each cake and each bake and she offered the woman to taste of each cake and each bake and the woman did taste them all and the woman did not even make that phone call, and it was not clear to her whether the woman had forgotten about the phone call since there were so many cakes and bakes to try or whether the woman had only come in to taste her cakes and bakes or perhaps, and that is not completely impossible, perhaps the woman came in to talk to her and the woman did talk to her and while the woman talked to her, the woman said that her cakes, yes the woman said that, she definitely heard the woman say that and the woman referred to her by name – and how did she know her name? – the woman said, V, your cakes make me happy. Your cakes make me happy, the woman said, she said. And she did not know what to say not because the words surprised her, and that is not surprising, that is not surprising to her because nothing surprises her these days but the real point of those words was that there was something definitive about them, something that did not allow anything else to be said. That is why the words stayed with her and she thought they were good words, undoubtedly good words, the words that were about her, the words that were prompted by her cakes and so she thought that perhaps, after all, cakes, or at least her cakes, could be about love. A few days after the woman had said V, your cakes make me happy, she was baking cakes, trying out new recipes, the cakes the woman had not tried before and she thought the woman might come in and try those new cakes, those new cakes the woman had not tried before, and she even thought that those new cakes would make the woman happy and that there could be something, something a little bit like love in that and she had many more cakes, and many more varieties than ever before when the woman had come round but the woman did not come. And the woman did not come a week later and there were so many cakes, too many to take to the ducks at the pond in Putney and so she threw them out. She threw the cakes out, lots of cakes, many different cakes. That was some time ago and she had not seen the woman for a while, for a year or two even, yes, two years it must be and she wondered what had happened to the woman, whether the woman's gentleman's friend had moved away or whether the relationship had not survived and so the woman had no reason to come to the street, she said, for really the woman came for the man, the man who was the woman's gentleman friend, and not for the cakes and now when she thinks about it, it occurs to her that that whole episode, that whole episode had a possibility of something, a friendship even, a possibility of cakes giving love. Did she mean giving love or getting love? She is not sure but there was something about love and those cakes. Now that she looks back to that episode she thinks of it as a failure – cake baking as a failure? – but even that is fine for she no longer needs to get love and she could never get love from women, the treacherous Eves, always pushing her in the paddling pool, like those girls when she was not yet four years old, women always luring her in, always that same pattern of turning up, calling attention to themselves, chasing her with love and then when she wants to give it back to them, when she wants to give love and have love, have their love, they take off, they disappear, they do not return her calls, they cut her out, they cut her out without a word. But not any more, she will not fall prey to their friendship, their false friendship, their temptations of friendship, and now her baking is about her, she tells herself, her baking is about her without love and without the need for love, her baking is about leaving that dark room, that room that always stays dark even when she remembers to put the light on and when she can be bothered to open the shutters. And the woman is not coming back, she is sure of that, the woman could have been run over, she could have had a heart attack, she could have been kidnapped, she could have emigrated, or perhaps she was one of those women who goes around sniffing in front of people's front doors and knocking on those doors when she could smell a cake and that woman must have been in the habit of doing that and perhaps there was no gentleman friend and all of that is possible but not important to her just as it is possible but not important to her that the woman simply got bored with the cakes and bakes. She does not care what the reason might be for the woman not coming back, nor does she care that she will never again see the woman for she knows that she does not like most people, in fact she doesn't like almost all the people, except for a very few, very few who know better than to meddle with others, with their baking and their cakes, she does not like people except for a very, very few who keep themselves to themselves, she does not like people with their habits and with their lack of habits. She bakes and bakes and she makes all those scones, sweet and savoury, herby and fruity, all those cakes and all those tarts that are too much for one person, she makes and bakes for no one, she makes and bakes to get it over with.

The Bottom Line

HE RANG THIS morning to say he'd be half an hour late. Now, that's a first. Normally, he's on the dot or early, even. He'll make it up to me, he said. Pay extra for the time.

I've lost count how many times he's been over the past two years. We meet once every couple of months. So, it must be around a dozen visits.

I like a regular. He's one of a few I have. You could say that there isn't much excitement in that, but I am not in the business for excitement. The arrangement works for both of us: we know what to expect and the routine we follow.

Usually, he rings a week before the appointment. It's always Thursday he wants, Thursday afternoon; it has to be after two o'clock. His wife has an aerobics class in the evening and comes back late. Anyway, that's what he told me. I never ask about their circumstances. If a punter wants Thursday afternoon, so long as I'm not booked, Thursday afternoon he shall have. I imagine if the wife comes home late on a Thursday, tired after aerobics, she makes no demands on him.

With him, it's always an in-call only. Most married ones ask for that, unless they have checked into a hotel. And he always wants two hours. I don't even ask. When he rings, all I say is 'The usual?' and he replies, 'Yes, thank you, Marcella.' With him saying my name: that sounds friendly. I know he likes to treat me well. Nice, you could say. Fair. And it shows we have known each other for some time. We are a team. Although, to tell you the truth, when push comes to shove, I don't care. I don't do this work for friendship. When he talks to me on the phone, I can almost see him with his serious face nodding. That's how well I know him.

Most of them are serious. It's only after a drink or two that I can make them laugh. Anxious, I suppose. Worried about their performance. I see through a punter like that straightaway. There's only one thing to do. It always works: just tell them how much you are going to enjoy being with them, show them that you like what they are doing to you. I moan, I scream, I fake orgasms. And what do they do? Lap it all up. I know they aren't stupid. Perhaps days or weeks later they think back and wonder whether it was really that great for me. But, never mind. The fact is that I relax them and make them feel good. Isn't that what they pay for? Making them feel good.

But he doesn't need relaxing. I don't think so. Nor do I need to fake. He isn't like the others: he doesn't expect me to have an orgasm. Just as well. He cares for me in a different sort of way; sometimes when we talk, I feel I could almost say something that didn't sound stupid.

I see him like Peter Pan, a boy who never grew up. I remember seeing the poster for the film. I went to see it a few years ago, with Myra. We were taking her son. Little Damian got angry when we read out the words on the poster to him. He wanted to grow up as quickly as possible, he said.

But not this man. However clever he might be, his visits to me are a refusal to grow up. He comes to me to make sure that he stays a little boy.

We do spend the entire two hours together. Some of them

leave, or want me to leave, as soon as they have finished. Guilt, probably.

When I open the door, he is standing there in his shabby brown jacket – all these years he always wears the same one – holding a crumpled carrier bag. I move aside to let him pass. We briefly smile at each other. He goes straight to my reception room and lowers himself on the sofa. He places an envelope with the money on the coffee table at the side. Yes, that's another thing that makes him different. The envelope. I don't look at it or put it away until he has left. I offer him a drink. I don't with others, but then, he is special. Yes, special. Well, I don't know how to describe it. But he is. It's always a beer he wants. I fetch it from the refrigerator in the kitchen – I have it chilled ready for him – and sit on a chair opposite him. I wait for him to start.

He takes a sip of the beer, asks how I am, and then has another sip. Next, he questions me about something that's in the news. Usually, I have no time to read the papers, but before he arrives, if I can at all manage, I do check the front page of the *Mail*. You have to make the effort. Preparation for the job. I want every punter to feel satisfied, let alone my regulars. You have to make it special for them.

What was it last time? Oh yes, something about nurses' pay. The first time we met, I didn't know what to say. Besides, some might take offence if you say something about a thing like that. Best to let them say whatever they want to say then nod and agree. How was I supposed to know what his views were? I have to deal with all sorts. I bet some of my clients would come to blows. People are so different. Except when it comes to sex. Most men are the same there.

So, I was both being careful and not quite sure what I

should say. But he took his time with me. He's a patient man. On that day he looked to me like a teacher. Perhaps he is one; I've never asked. Anyway, he explained to me what the dispute was about. I did think then that if only my teachers at school had been so patient with me. If only they had been like him, speaking slowly, without making me feel stupid. If only they had made sure that I had understood.

I don't know why he wants to talk to me about such serious things. None of the other guys do. I bet he has lots of friends to discuss what's in the papers with. At first, I used to find it tedious. I didn't care what he was saying. But then his manner, that patient, slow way of explaining, won me over. These days I even look forward to his questions. Well, sort of. It makes a difference from the usual conversations.

We talk about whatever he reads out to me, either from a magazine, or a newspaper, or sometimes even from a book. That's what he has in that carrier bag. Something to read. To read out aloud, to read to me. And then he looks at me and waits for me to say something. I have learned that nothing happens unless I make a comment, no matter how brief. The word that he often uses is exploitation. He says, 'Marcella, the world is full of those who exploit and those who are exploited. In our system, all relationships are about exploitation.'

So, if my mind wanders a bit or what he reads is difficult to follow, and I'm at a loss what to say, it seems I can't go wrong if I mention that word. As soon as I say it, his face lights up. That's the teacher in him: his pupil is doing well and he's proud. As for me, I always remember what old Miss Joanna said to me when I started working for her: 'This business is part of the service industry. You are here to please.'

Another time he read out something about men not

helping women with housework. He wanted me to comment. The word exploitation seemed to fit, and he was pleased. But I didn't agree with him. In my opinion, any woman who shacks up with a man should expect to do the housework. That's how men are. You can't change them. My mother had to put up with a lazy drunkard until she couldn't take it any more and threw him out. That's why I'm my own woman.

So, we have a little talk. But as soon as I've answered the question, he launches into an explanation. 'The problem is about . . .' he says. So, with the nurses, he said that their union was not as powerful as the doctors' and that was because they were mostly women, while doctors were mostly men, so the nurses were bound to be paid less. Again, I wasn't sure I agreed: doctors are cleverer as well, they can do things nurses can't. I keep quiet and nod from time to time while he talks. He doesn't mind that I don't ask questions at that point; the last time he said he was pleased how well I listened. Well, sometimes I'm almost interested in what he says, but if I'm not, I just remember that I'm part of the service industry. As long as I nod, I can think my own thoughts.

Last week he read me an article about women working in textile factories in India and how little they were paid. 'Marcella,' he said, 'coming here on the bus, I looked at people's feet. Half of them were wearing trainers. I wondered how many of them were made in places like the Philippines, where the wages are very low and the factory owners and their western masters are making huge profits.'

I was thinking of Lia, the Philippine girl who lives in the flat below mine. She does a bit of work for Miss Joanna's massage parlour and she says that the oldest and the dirtiest men who come in are always given to her. I know that's the pecking order at the establishment. She has no work permit, she has to keep quiet. There's no good arguing with Miss Joanna. So I got interested when he told me about the Indian women and the trainers. But he had to go and we never finished the conversation. I must tell him today that it's not just the trainers. I'll tell him about Lia.

The conversation takes approximately half of the time he spends here. Once he has finished his talk, he asks me a question or two, usually to check how much I've understood and then, very gently, he stands up, puts his hands together, looks at me and says, 'I am ready now.'

'Good,' I say. At this point, my voice sounds rough and determined.

I walk to the bedroom and he follows. Now, I'm fully in charge. I sit in the armchair and ask him to kneel down in front of me. He obeys immediately.

'Kiss my shoes,' I shout.

He covers them with urgent kisses.

'The soles as well,' I shout and he carries on until I order him to stop.

Then I ask him whether he has been a naughty boy.

'Yes, Miss. Very naughty,' he whispers, his eyes on the floor.

'Then you deserve to be punished.'

He starts shaking. I order him to pull his trousers down and kneel against the bed. He does.

'That's no good,' I shout. 'You naughty boy, you must present your naked bottom for me to deal with.' With no hesitation, his hands yank down his underpants.

'Lift the bottom,' I order. 'Higher, higher, now, that's better.'

I take a cane and swish it through the air. I can see his buttocks stiffen with anticipation. Then I swing it again and make it land on his bottom. He utters a sigh. I go on, increasing the force of the hit with each move. Red streaks appear on his skin. His breathing is deep and loud, mouth wide open. In between my strokes, he screams, 'More, more, I've been very naughty,' and I oblige. The skin breaks and drops of blood dot his buttocks. My cane smears them around; red treacle makes its way down a buttock and the back of the thigh.

Now he is panting loudly, his body stiffens, his back convulses back and forth and there he is: ejaculating. I stand by and watch him. He collapses on the bed, his breathing still loud.

'Marcella, you are an angel. This was wonderful.'

'I do what I can,' I say.

'Oh, Marcella, you surpassed yourself this time. It gets better and better.'

I thank him.

'Could you pass me a mirror?'

I have it ready.

He turns so that his back is reflected in the wardrobe mirror and then holds the one I have just given him in front of him so that he can catch the reflection. His cock begins to stiffen again and he sighs. I always make sure that one of the lines is particularly deep and prominent. I hit in the same place again and again. He runs the tip of his finger along the deepest cut and the breathing intensifies. The second coming.

Then it's a few minutes of absolute stillness, with him lying on his side, eyes closed. At this point, he likes me to lie next to him, my arm around his back. I remain fully clothed. When he opens his eyes, he smiles at me, and he says something about our initial discussion. Something like, 'Remember, Marcella, those factory workers in the Far East, we have to help them. It's a small world; we all depend on one another.'

I agree with that. I depend on him making these visits.

He arrives exactly half an hour late, as he said he would. Immediately, I notice that he has no carrier bag. Perhaps a book, or a journal, is stuffed inside his jacket pocket. I watch as he makes his way to the front room, places an envelope on the coffee table and sits down. I remind myself to tell him about Lia.

He doesn't want a drink. Something is wrong. I wait.

'Marcella, we need to talk,' he says. His face is gloomy. Has the wife found out?

'What have you got today? What are you going to read?' I try to show enthusiasm.

'I am not going to read.' It must be because he's late and has to leave that part out.

'Shall we go to the bedroom straightaway?'

He takes a deep breath, looks down and then back at me.

'I've thought a great deal about my visits. As you know, I have always enjoyed them. And I've developed certain feelings, well, how shall I put it, I've developed a caring attitude towards you. I've also realised that what I'm doing is not right. I've been exploiting you. The business you are in is about men using their economic power and exploiting women like you. I've been hypocritical. I have been showing you how people exploit others while, at the same time, I've been exploiting you. I've been exploiting you and that has to stop. That is the bottom line. I feel terrible about it. I've come to apologise. I'm really ashamed of myself. Please forgive me, Marcella.'

He stands up to go.

I don't know what to think.

'So you don't want to, you don't want me to spank you?'

He looks at me: 'I've left some money, a bit more than usual. To make it up for future lost wages.' He walks towards the door.

'Good luck, Marcella. Remember our conversations. You must not allow anyone to exploit you.'

I'm left alone. Should I have seen it coming? After all, he has always been a bit strange. Well, as old Joanna says, 'You win some, you lose some.' Perhaps it was the routine that he was getting bored with. In this business, they always want something new. If only he had asked. If only he had asked.

My next appointment is not until this afternoon. I have some time for myself until then. Perhaps I'll pop down and see Lia, have a cup of coffee with her.

The Temptation of St Anthony

H E LOVED BOOKS. He read books. He collected books.

He had friends who wrote books.

Books were his life.

One day he wrote a book. And another. And another.

His three-bedroom home was full of books, or that's what people said. But people say all sorts of things. Occasionally, he heard them and thought how sloppy the world was when it came to using language. Most people exaggerated, out of laziness or to achieve effect. They bandied with words as if their speech was of no consequence. Had his home really been full of books, it would not have been possible to bring in one more book. That clearly was not the case. Every day he added another book or two, or three, and sometimes even more, to his collection. His library blossomed in its eternal spring. Books lined all his walls. Books double-lined, triple-lined all his walls. The smallest of the bedrooms was full of books. He could no longer step in. That was no problem. It was a guest bedroom and he rarely had anyone staying with him overnight. On the rare occasions he would be required to offer a bed to a late visitor or an acquaintance from another city, he reasoned, they could be accommodated in his study on a chaise longue.

'He can't resist them,' someone said.

'He always gives in,' someone else said.

Mea culpa, I thought, remembering gifting him the books.

'His place looks like a cave; I caught a glimpse of it the other day,' yet someone else said.

He heard them but paid no attention. They understood nothing. He was living his life.

As he acquired more books, he stacked them on tables, chairs, and then deposited them on the floor of the lounge. With time, the lounge too became impassable. The sun could no longer penetrate its windows as the glass was blocked by columns of books piled up to the ceiling.

When more book acquisitions poured in, he stored them in the study. It was only a matter of a year and a few months before the chaise longue disappeared under a pile of books. Soon after, the room could no longer be entered. But there was no cause to worry. He couldn't remember the last occasion anyone paid him a visit, let alone when anyone expected to be put up for the night. Nor did he need a separate study. After all, most of the time he worked in his bedroom.

What pure joy to live with books. Was there anything else he could possibly want?

Love? Yes, but love is precarious. Love hurts. Love betrays. No, not love.

One day he pushed his bed into the space between the bathroom and the kitchen door. Writing was important to him; he didn't have to remind himself of that. Nor did he have to remind himself that he was not getting any younger. There were still all those books to read, all those books to write. What was the point of wasting time moving from the kitchen to the bedroom and then to the bathroom, whenever his biological needs demanded? A smaller living space would allow him to concentrate on what was important.

With the bed in its new position, the toilet and the fridge

were only a step away. In fact, he realised, the situation could be further improved: he didn't need the fridge. Not for food. He switched it off. Its interior provided extra shelving space for books. The tins of soup that furnished his meals could be kept anywhere, by the foot of his mattress, on the top of the toilet cistern. He loved working from his bed.

In no time, his bedroom, his former bedroom, and then the kitchen and the rest of the corridor were stuffed with books. When the corridor was filled, except for a narrow access to the front door, he placed the books on the mattress. He slept curled up like a foetus. The position was comforting and did not require much space. When more books dropped through the letter box, he placed them under the pillow, on the pillow next to his face and around his curled-up frame. One day the pile by the front door reached the level of the letter box and blocked it. But the postman was a diligent worker and a strong man with hard biceps, a former weight-lifting champion. He recognised a challenge when he saw one. He made every effort to push new arrivals through and dislodged the blockage once, twice, again and again. Each time, he slapped his hands in satisfaction and smiled.

The books crawled onto the man's body. One day the postman lost his strength and despite his conscientious attitude to his work, he could not carry out the delivery. Whatever books he carried in his bag had to be returned to the sorting office. Nothing could go through the mail slot on the front door. Not even the slimmest volume of poetry, not a single sheet carrying a story.

The postman felt he was not up to his job any more. He took early retirement.

The man on the bed dreamt of a country with no name,

no borders, no single language. A country like a symphony of words. A country like his library. All absorbing. A country that contained the world. He dreamt.

He had always known that we learn to live from books but it came to him as a welcome surprise that we learn to die from books too.

They found him one day.

An elegant cranium lay on top of two polished clavicles, next to a basilica of neat ribs, a well-shaped sacrum and graceful femurs, a pair of tibias and fibulas. The humerus, radius and ulnas shone porcelain-white, in death, his skeleton fragile like life. But the books, the books he had read, the books he had written, the books that were gifted to him, the books lived on, eloquent and powerful. The books tell his story.

First Words of Love

In memory of Antun Gustav Matoš (1873–1914)

FOR THE PAST twenty minutes, I have been sitting quietly, avoiding their eyes. On these journeys, I isolate myself as soon as I find a seat. Most people on this route are middle aged or elderly, often alone, and they seek someone to talk to. I make sure I take a book out and although the act of reading would make me nauseous, I hold it in front of my face to discourage a conversation. When the tram jerks to a halt at the final stop, my fellow passengers jostle towards the exit, restless and impatient as if their lives depended on how quickly they move on. In years to come I will begin to understand the need to treat death with urgency. But unlike for them, for me this trip is not about death. It is about love.

I watch them crowd the bus station, a hundred metres away, and from a distance they merge into a dark, amorphous blob that sticks to the glass sides of the shelter. Not for a second do I consider joining them; the sight of their wobbly bodies makes me uncomfortable and I cannot wait to be away from their shrill voices and those raucous bursts of laughter. Even on the way to the cemetery they cannot keep quiet. I must learn to shut out all those sensations that distract me from serious thought. And today especially I need time and solitude to prepare my heart. I continue on my journey uphill, along the long wide pavement, lined with centuries-old oaks, heavily pollarded into sturdy minimalist sculptures, when I notice with satisfaction that now there is no human being in sight. The air is quiet enough for me to think and choose the words that I want to say and that I want to hear. He and I know that words are too important to be left to the chance of the moment. As I compose sentences, listen to phrases, saying them aloud, I nurture the anticipation of our meeting.

The sun is low on the horizon; there is still an hour before it disappears and I pause for a moment, taking pleasure in the strong, blindingly white light that makes the landscape around me look unreal. In my book, unreal means uplifting and I inhale deeply, filling my lungs with the thin, crisp air until I feel dizzy, drunk with excitement and desire. But soon that sensation turns into a longing, that feeling inside my chest, that intermittent pain, too elusive to be defined, but perhaps like a flutter of a bird with a broken wing, a bird thrashing about desperately, while willing its brain to lift its body hopelessly tied to the ground. I have known that longing since the preceding spring when I was about to be thirteen and by now I am all too familiar with the melancholy it brings. In years to come, it will stay with me, losing its intensity every now and then, and, as I grow older, I imagine I shall embrace its occasional revisit as a welcome memory of youth.

But today the longing distracts me and, despite my efforts to refocus my thoughts, the memories of yesterday take over. I hear my parents asking why I cannot be like everyone else. 'Why don't you go skating? And call him.' I walk faster, I am almost running, catching my breath. I need to shake off the world of the family and their demands. None of that matters, I tell myself. Think of what is important. Soon I will be with the man I love; why should I care about anything else? We shall talk about things that are important: writing, love.

At some point I might say those words, and I know I won't help smiling at that point, and then, I am sure, we will both laugh. Yes, I will say that I have come *per pedes apostolorum*. I will say the words slowly, enjoying their sound, as I always do, proud of our private allusion. Like all lovers, we have our secrets. And in our heads we shall hear the sonnet where he used the phrase; that's where I have learned it from. I know most of his poems by heart; I recite them when I am alone, and sometimes to him as well. He hasn't said so but I know that it gives him pleasure to hear his words from my mouth. From time to time, I ask him about music and his cello playing in the city's orchestra, but on that I have little to say; I am tone deaf. I sense that he is too kind to comment on my poor knowledge of music.

I see him only once a week, but he is with me all the time; I never stop thinking about him. And I talk to him all the time, sometimes quietly in my head, other times aloud, conjuring his presence even though he is far away. There is no one whose opinions I value more and that is why he is the first person, often the only person, I consult about any decisions I have to make. His photograph stands in a frame at my bedside; last night, as every night, I kissed it before switching off the light and then, lying in complete darkness, a feeling of warmth, satiny warmth, surged through my body. I whispered: 'See you tomorrow.' Oh, what bliss it was. The warmth, the warmth, the warmth and then . . . there was lightness and . . . and I could fly.

When I awoke, it was still dark outside but I could see him already working, hunched over his desk. When he finished, he turned towards me: 'Tell me what you think,' he said, passing me a sheaf of pages covered in handwriting.

'They want it for tomorrow's edition.' The piece started with his review of an art exhibition and then moved onto wider issues of the artist's social responsibility, citing Voltaire and Rousseau and Zola. It's not the first time he has referred to them; I had taken note and have started to read their work: I love that I have so much to learn from him, and not only in literature and art. There is philosophy, and politics too. And music: the cello is my favourite instrument and, despite what I think of as my handicap, he guides my taste. He is perfect. Just perfect.

I cannot deny that his looks are important to me. Without doubt, he is more attractive than any other man I can think of. Although he is not unusually tall, his figure is reminiscent of Picasso's *Don Quixote*. I think of him as lean and fragile, but also sharp and pointed, needle-like – he used the phrase in his short story 'The Needle Brat'. No wonder he is slim after all those years he spent in Paris, living the life of a poet in a shabby garret, eating meagre rations in cafés, absconding from one place to another whenever he couldn't pay the rent. He has written about those years of his youth and so have others. As he has aged, his body has become slightly stooped and when he walks, his eyes focus on the ground in front of his feet. I love that look when he is alone, the serious demeanour, the face of a man self-sufficient in his world. The look of a man focused on what is important: words. And I love his gaunt features, his angular cheeks, the head that is shaped as if it has been chiselled by a sculptor. (In time to come, I will think of Giacometti.) I love his thin hands with fingers elongated from years stretching to reach the strings of the cello. But above all, I love his passion, the animation of his speech. And then there is his voice with its distinctive colour: I would recognise it in a chorus of millions. I could never love a man whose voice does not speak to me as special.

I have been in love with him for a year and what a wonderful year it has been. How lucky I am to have found him, an intellectual soul mate, a teacher and a lover. As spring emerges and the days begin to stretch, it will be easier to make my weekly trips; I will not have to set out so early to avoid the walk back in the dark, when the neighbourhood acquires a threatening mood. Even during the day, there are few people around his lodgings. It is much busier on Sundays when parents take their children for afternoon walks. At the beginning of the nineteenth century the area used to be the private garden of an aristocratic family. Although the land now belongs to the public, and many more people have moved in, there is still something unique about the place. Perhaps it's to do with the classical architecture, the numerous sculptures and works of art spread around the park, or with the well-established hedges and giant cedar trees growing inside the ivy-covered walls. There are more flowers blooming in the well-tended beds than in any other part of the town. And the views from the hill over the city are unforgettable, without a doubt the best in the area. The long-term residents must be so used to the beauty of the place that they take it for granted, never commenting on it.

As I reach the promontory, a little square with the huts of flower sellers and the stalls of candle makers set out in a semicircle, I notice that, for the first time this year, they have daffodils and bluebells. I hesitate for a few moments before making the same choice as always: red roses, the symbol of love. He loves them best, of course he does; he is a poet.

As soon as I collect the bouquet and turn to go, I hear

someone calling my name, once, twice, the second time more loudly. I cannot tell where the voice is coming from. There are a few people around now but no one is looking at me. Then I hear someone running and I feel a hand on my shoulder. 'I wasn't sure it was you,' he says. He is a year or two above me at school but I cannot remember his name. Pavel? We were in the same play once and a month later I saw him at a birthday party. I was leaving early and he suddenly turned up by the door and said he was going the same way. How did he know what the same way was? On the bus, he said I should come to see a film with him; he mentioned a title and I could tell straightaway it wasn't a film I would like. He didn't even know the name of the director. I wouldn't bother with films on general release; I watch films only at the *cinémathèque*. I didn't tell him that; after all, he is one of the crowd. And how could I have explained to him that, in the cinema, I have to be alone. I pretend that strangers are not there and shut them out, but to go with a boy like him, that wouldn't be possible. I have dreamed of booking the entire auditorium and sitting there completely alone, obliterating the world outside the screen. Perhaps I should have told him; it might have put him off.

'Fancy seeing you here,' he says, smiling. His eyes dance. 'I'm off to a party. Come with me.'

What can I say?

'The roses are nice. Who are they for?'

What can I say?

The red roses. Did he give them to his fiancée? People have written about her: younger than him, rather prim, a school teacher. Olga. Yes, it was Olga who broke the engagement; what an unkind thing to do, abandon him when he needed her most. After the operation, he had no voice and when friends visited him in hospital, he would write them notes on scraps of paper. Some of them were written to Olga. She must have been a woman with no heart. How awful. I could never walk away from someone I loved when they needed me most. His life would have been so different had I, rather than Olga, that selfish woman, been with him at the time.

'Wait, don't go away. I'll come with you.'

How can I make him leave me alone? It's best to ignore him and avoid explanations.

'What's wrong? Vesna, why don't you say something?'

'I . . .' No. Nothing to say. Walk away. Fast.

I carry the red roses in my arms, closely pressed to my chest, their scent rising to my nostrils. I know the way from the main road to his place like the back of my hand. It is straight down for a few minutes, and then near the benches, by an old oak, there is a pathway on the right. And there he is. I see him in the distance. My heart beats faster and heat rises through my body; my cheeks are flushed. I wonder if my pupils have dilated? I have read somewhere that this happens at the moment of orgasm.

I am a woman in love.

As always, he is waiting for me. Although he does not say anything, I know that he is pleased to see me. His place needs tidying up. Before anything else, I deal with the prac-ticalities and throw out the old flowers, pour clean water in the vase and arrange the new bouquet. There. Elegant, long stalks. The crimson petals holding errant drops of water. He doesn't bother with housekeeping, preferring to wait for me. Perhaps, when it comes to women, he is a bit old-fashioned. But I don't mind. Not in the least. I understand it: he is older than me, a product of a culture that regarded women as weak and gentle, home-makers. I am more than happy to indulge him.

As soon as I put the vase away, I notice that we are not alone. There is a man visiting my poet, standing still and watching me. I have not met him before but recognise him from the pictures in the poet's biographies. In life, he looks stockier and shorter but the face is familiar: this old man in his late sixties is my lover's nephew. I feel his eyes on me, eyes that wonder, eyes that want to ask questions. When I return his gaze, I am greeted with a look of admiration, a look with no words, a look that renders me self-conscious. But he has a kind face. I am about to speak. He is quicker:

'I have seen you here before. You are very young.' I don't think so, but to a man of his age, a girl of fourteen is young. But none of that is important. Here is a member of my love's family and I am glad to meet him. The eyes of the man do not move from me.

'It makes me happy to see that young people today like his work.' He pauses – and it is a long pause – before adding, 'I came to it rather late.' I know that too. The nephew lived abroad with his mother, an international opera singer, and, as a child, would have known his uncle only briefly.

'I was only ten when . . .', the man says.

I nod: the dates are indelibly imprinted in my memory. I do not have to look at the inscriptions on the stone in front of me. My poet lover was born on the thirteenth of June 1873 and he died on the seventeenth of March 1914, more than forty years before I was born.

Futures

TANYA HAD WONDERED about her over the years. Ten years inside gives you lots of time to think. A couple of the women she met were like Sarah, clever busybodies. The call came out of the blue. Sarah's voice sounded familiar but it took Tanya a while to work out who it was. Sarah was chatty as if nothing had happened in the last thirty years and they could pick up where they left off. It should be clear to Sarah that Tanya was no longer a 'confused young woman', her lawyer's words. Tanya didn't recognise that description of herself, but perhaps that's how others would have seen her. Whatever she was then, now she is the Director of Futures. Sarah rang her because she saw an online article about the project. What did she google? 'Former prostitute'?

Sarah said she wanted them to meet. She runs an art gallery, in north-east London. She asked how Tanya was – she was doing a job, there was nothing else to say; she wasn't married – and then talked about herself.

Tanya has hardly done any work all morning, nervous about the meeting. She could speak to Sarah all right but she remembers how her brain used to freeze whenever she met those students. Today she will have to guard against that. After all, she is forty-nine, and director of an organisation that matters. They are a small charity, eight women and her, but they are doing important work and she is used to dealing with important people. She has been twice to 10 Downing Street;

been invited to talk to ministers; organised fund-raising galas; has met celebrities. She has her professional role and respect. But that woman could turn her back into a twenty-year-old street-walker, lost for words, doing what she wants her to do.

Unable to work, Tanya has been drawing. Now she has two new pastels, one of the daffodils in a vase on the table and another of the blue hyacinths in a pot on the window ledge. They could be presents for her visitor. No, she wouldn't do that. Sarah might say how lovely they were and she couldn't bear to be patronised. She'll see all the stuff hanging around – she could hardly miss the dozens of frames covering the office walls – but Tanya won't admit that she did them. She's improved after more than twenty years of using pencils, charcoal and pastels, producing thousands of pictures. There were people who liked them, which was useful in prison where she could exchange them for favours, a haircut or manicure. But she isn't an artist; pretty pictures do not move her. Her drawings were more useful: they were her midwife, helping her give birth to a different Tanya. They are small, drawn on sheets from an A4 sketchbook; they don't take long to complete. Drawing takes her out of the self she doesn't want to be. When she traces the outline of a petal, she is there, on the leaves, her mind focused on the flower. When she comes back, she is clear headed and she can do whatever she needs.

Throughout the trial, she was numbed. The prosecution claimed she had shown no remorse. But she had felt dissociated from the person who had killed Dave and from the person on trial. After she was sentenced to life imprisonment, the real anger kicked in. She was ferocious, livid, attacking her solicitor and her welfare officer. They put her on medication for two years. Chemical imprisonment. In the second year, she made friends with two women, one of them a prostitute, and talking with them she realised how her whole life had been one of abuse, first by her mother and her lovers and then by Dave and the punters. A long time passed before she had agreed to counselling. She was angry with the therapist, losing her rag in every session. One day the therapist came in with a sketchpad, pencils and a flower pot. As soon as Tanya started screaming, she stopped the session and they both drew the flowers. That helped. She drew at every session and she started drawing before and after the sessions; soon she was drawing whenever she felt anger moving its head, which was pretty much most days.

This morning she dressed carefully, more formally than she would for an ordinary day at the office: this isn't an ordinary day. Her past is coming back into her life and she mustn't let it take over her present. She needs to show that ex-student that she's no longer the pathetic whore who needs help, bruised by her boyfriend, turning up at that silly consciousness-raising group. She is the Director of Futures; that's why Sarah is coming. She repeats that in her head again and again as if it's her who needs reminding. She considered her new M&S grey flannel dress, or the red Wallis skirt that makes her feel elegant, but in the end she opted for a dark trouser suit and high heels – her confidence outfit. Her short hair's completely grey these days, but that's fine. People show more respect to older women. She'll keep her glasses on all the time – even though she's short-sighted and anything near will be out of focus. She knows how important it is to project the right image; she has been on courses.

They are meeting on her territory: a clear advantage. She opens the window overlooking the street – a quiet cul-de-sac

– to air her office for the visitors. Sarah's on time. Tanya moves to the window and hears Sarah climb the stairs leading to the front door and press the bell. She hears Carol downstairs telling Sarah that Ms Davies is in the gallery. The joke about her office confuses visitors and sometimes she tells the receptionists to be more helpful but today she is pleased: Sarah's not the only one with a gallery. The visitor stops at the door of Tanya's office and Tanya looks up from the papers in her hand, pretending that she's been working. She has a second or two to take in what Sarah looks like: she doesn't think she would have recognised her on the street. The two decades have taken their toll but, if anything, she looks even more posh. Tanya stands up and extends her hand. That's how she greets her visitors, the government people and the like. Sarah takes her by surprise and, still holding her hand, embraces her, holds her tight and kisses her on both cheeks. 'Tanya, you look great.'

And then Sarah talks about the past and says how wonderful that consciousness-raising group was as it brought women together and Tanya thinks of that disastrous consciousness raising-group run by those students who had no idea about her life and she has to focus to stay in control. She mustn't forget that they are not back in Birmingham. Tanya points to the armchairs in the corner of her office and makes coffee – the next stage in the standard routine – and once they're both seated and the coffee is poured, she tries to think of Sarah as her project partner. There are lots of those; no organisation on its own could meet the needs of women trying to escape prostitution. Her visitors fall into two groups: those who make her work possible – grant-giving organisations, journalists, government people, drugs charities, health workers – and those she can help – the prostitutes. She tells Sarah about the charity, gives her leaflets and then she has nothing else to say. What's this visit about? Then Sarah asks about prison and she doesn't mind telling her, but why does this woman want to hear it? She must know it from the article. The facts, what the journalists called facts. But not all facts. No one knows that it was the first time in her life that she had felt safe. But she doesn't tell her that. Sarah talks about her life, mentions several other women from the group that she still keeps in touch with, talks about their children and then asks: 'What about your girl? She could be thirty. Are you a grandmother yet?'

'Lilla was adopted. It was best at the time. We aren't in touch.' That's the truth. But the whole truth is that at the time she couldn't have cared less what happened. That's how angry she was. And now the whole truth is that whenever a prostitute in her early thirties comes to Futures, Tanya hopes, she hopes to God, that it's not her daughter. She stares at the young women, assessing their facial features, their figures, their hair, thinking whether anything reminds her of Lilla. Perhaps that's what drives her: her delayed maternal instinct. She is working to save those women from themselves, as if they are all her daughters. She tells them it's not too late; it wasn't too late for her. Often they don't believe her but at least a few try.

She mustn't say more and so she stands up busying herself with the blind – the sun is shining directly into the eyes of her visitor. 'A nice afternoon; it didn't rain after all,' Tanya says. Sarah should be ready to leave. There is nothing else to say. And what's been said is of no use to anyone.

Sarah stands up and peers closely at the pictures on the walls. 'You draw. Amazing. All those on the staircase.

Hundreds of them.' Tanya remembers that she has forgotten to hide the two pastels she did this morning. Too late to lie. 'You have an assured hand,' Sarah says. 'The charcoals on the stairs are marvellous. I admired the technique.' She picks up the pastels from the desk and smiles. 'It's the discrepancy between the realism of the lines and the surrealism of the colour schemes, like here, amazing, blue daffodils with red leaves. That's witty.' Sarah could always talk, like everyone in that group. 'Yeees,' she says, still holding the 'witty' pastels. She must think they are crap. She walks around the office, commenting on individual pictures, her voice light and happy and it occurs to Tanya that perhaps she's being unfair to her visitor. 'Tanya,' Sarah says. 'I don't know what to say.' Tanya laughs. That's not possible but something in her makes her think: serves you right. Isn't that how she had felt all those years ago?

Then Carole comes knocking on the door: 'The police have raided a brothel and arrested a group of men running a trafficking ring; it's big news and that journalist wants to have the interview ready earlier.'

She can manage that. Like the journalist, she has to make use of the moment: the arrest is a big story. Sarah wants to know more. Tanya goes into her explaining gear and tells her that now that prostitution is increasingly seen as part of the entertainment industry, the only real sympathy most people feel is for the women who are trafficked. That's still unacceptable. Even punters say – but can you believe a man who buys a woman? – they wouldn't do it if they knew the woman had been trafficked. Tanya believes the distinction doesn't mean much. It overlooks the fact that there is always an element of force. Trafficked women have it harder – they are cheated directly – consenting to one thing and then being forced to do something else, but she too was forced, cheated. At the age of ten, she had no idea what those men were about, her mother's friends, buying her ice creams and checking whether she was warm enough. The same with Dave. A pimp, not a boyfriend. She couldn't see that then. She was forced because she had no choice. She didn't know there could be a choice. And these days, they do drugs much more. A woman who is a drug addict has no choice.

'What's the answer, what's the solution?' Sarah asks.

'Abolish prostitution.'

'Make it illegal?'

'Yes, but criminalise the men, not the women.' She should have been more precise. For women pay for sex too. Sex tourism, the abuse of their racial and economic power over local men. 'The women need help, they want to get out. I said to a minister the other day: 'Abolish poverty and there would be no supply. Until then, criminalise demand.'

Now her visitor is truly speechless. She can see that Sarah is thinking about what she has just heard.

Eventually Sarah stands up to leave. She invites Tanya to visit her gallery. 'We could do something together. A project. Art as therapy. I'd like to help,' Sarah says. Futures relies on volunteers. Posh women help with this sort of work. And she might even visit the gallery. See what pictures Sarah likes.

My Friend Karl

MY FRIEND KARL has a partner and a lover. He is devoted to both and willingly juggles his life around fixed weekly appointments with each of them. That requires some skill and sacrifice on his part. Neither of the women knows of the other's existence. Over the years, I have observed Karl as his partner and his lover unfailingly take holidays at the same time (not in the same place). Their timing amuses me but Karl, my friend whose life and home are more disorganised than any other I know, and who therefore insists on the regularity of his meetings with everyone, and with the two women in particular, as a way of keeping chaos at bay, must some time wish that the two women's absences were not so well coordinated and that he would be able to spend time with one of them without all that careful juggling. I have noticed that he feels at a loss about what to do with his suddenly acquired free time. I know that he treats himself to meals out and sits alone in restaurants with a book in front of him, reading until his food is served. I have also noticed – but this is not something I would tell him as I am sure he would deny it – that, during those weeks of his women's holidays, Karl, a renowned *flâneur* in his youth, shows a spring in his step. I imagine time flows at his bidding. I know for sure his sleep is sounder than ever and his inspiration to pen a verse or two is rekindled. I think that is important as he dreams that one day he will write a series of poems about his life and loves. 'Vita et Amores,' he said with a smile. 'I've already thought of the title.'

I love my friend Karl and last week when once again he said, with sadness in his voice, that both of his women were away at the same time, I suggested he try to influence their future holiday plans and avoid the situation. I repeated the suggestion this morning when I saw him sitting alone in the sunshine at a café down the road from me. 'But can't you see,' he said with a relaxed gesture of his hand, reminiscent of the man who smokes in Brecht, 'that is precisely what I have been doing for years. It takes some effort and, I assure you, all my skill, to coordinate their departures and arrivals.'

Telling Tales

THE SUMMER I separated from my husband, I rented a house in a remote hamlet in the Languedoc. It was a small, sparsely furnished cottage, painted white, with a door in the middle and a window on each side, surrounded by trellises and strands of old greenery, which knobbled its way around the wooden shutters, very much a house a child would draw. It nestled at the end of a narrow, country road with no shops, not even the ubiquitous boulangerie, in its immediate vicinity. Windows at the front and back offered views of vineyards stretching to the horizon. The solitary location of the house might have made it undesirable to the regular holiday renter and the owner readily agreed to offer it at a considerably reduced rate, marked down even further when, in response to his question – I had not contemplated the duration of my stay – I said I was planning to live there for at least six months, possibly a year. In fact, at the time, I had no thoughts about the next day and remaining in that house till the end of my life was not something I would have excluded had I spared a thought about the future. Once I arrived, the idea of ending my days in the area became attractive: the location of the cemetery was the most pleasing I had ever seen, peaceful with a marvellous view. The dead need little else.

The rental had been advertised in a literary journal. I contacted the proprietor on the spur of the moment. Although I had harboured no previous desire to move, let alone to up sticks to the French countryside, we completed all arrangements within a day via a few emails. Despite having only a vague notion of what the area was like, it didn't occur to me to ask any questions of the owner. Nor was I, a thoroughly urban creature, assailed by qualms about spending time alone in the countryside with no neighbours in sight and the prospect of not seeing anyone for days on end.

I had been known as a sociable person, and some people have occasionally referred to me as a party animal, a designation that was either the effect of my carefully constructed public persona or of people's inability to see beyond it. But truly, I was a loner, a person who felt most comfortable on my own. I lived in my head. I craved solitude, like some people crave a lover or a doughnut. But had anyone wished to look for patterns and links between my myriad selves – not something that would interest me in the least – they might explain my renting a French cottage as a subconscious (oh, how I wince at that word) expression of some part of me that didn't seem to have been perceived by the world at large.

You might be guessing that I sought solitude because I needed to get myself back on track, as people usually say. But the idea never crossed my mind. Nor do I remember the separation from my husband being overly traumatic, not in the sense that would make me avoid human contact. As far as I could tell, my departure for France was a random decision; it was mere coincidence that it followed closely upon the end of my marriage. But then, there are always people who try to establish links between our actions and whatever they can imagine exists in our past, or even our subconscious.

A few people amongst the small group of those I called friends were concerned about my impending departure and the question on everyone's lips seemed to be about 'what was I going to do there? Wouldn't I miss London?' At first, in order to allay their fears, I attempted to offer an explanation of how I envisaged my life alone in France – not that I had thought about it at all – but once I rattled off a plausible plan a couple of times, and answered questions, always the same questions, I felt a slight resentment at having to go through the ritual of justifying myself. The problems my friends voiced had to do with them rather than with me. While I felt neither fear nor excitement about leaving England for an unspecified period, possibly for good, and cutting myself off from everyone I knew, my friends found the idea alien to their own sensibilities. 'I couldn't do it, not at my age', or 'You are bound to be lonely, desperately lonely,' 'But this is where you belong' were the unsolicited comments I heard again and again. Even 'Why France?' But after a few days I learned that the best response – the only one that kept everyone happy – was simply to shrug and smile in a way that was meant to be both teasing and mysterious. It didn't stop them repeating the same worries but at least it allowed me to cope without becoming angry with them. After all, my life was none of their business. Some of them might have cared for me but that didn't mean they should interfere. I had neither dependants nor debts. I was free to go away whenever I liked. Free to go and not come back.

There was no reason for me to plan what I would do in Languedoc. The same as in London. Read and write. Think. Take long walks. Think. Watch old films. (The owner had told me that there was a vast collection of French DVDs; in fact, without me being aware of it, that piece of information might have made me rent the place without much consideration of anything else.) Looking back at the time before I left, I feel

I ought to stress that I wasn't tired of London. Even if that had been the case, Dr Johnson's warning – now, that was a character who regularly intrigued me – would have stopped me from admitting it to myself. Equally, I wasn't fleeing from anything or anyone.

Encumbered with neither fears nor hopes, I settled in easily. The house was sparsely furnished with simple, functional pieces, in the style that I would later learn was unusual for the rural Languedoc. Telephone and internet connection were sporadic but that suited me fine. On the kitchen table I found a brief note held down by a set of car keys, telling me that I was welcome to make use of the old Saab parked to the side of the house. I had already been told of a couple of bicycles in the garage and had thought they would be useful for my trips to a nearby village for the weekly market, one of those colourful local affairs, serving as much as an occasion for social gatherings as a place selling provisions and all kinds of necessities and unnecessities. Not that I expected to need much apart from pulses, nuts and dried fruit, both easily obtained in that part of the world and helpfully non-perishable.

Two months after my arrival, I received an email from a woman called Maya. The message would have been sitting in my inbox for a while since we had had a storm that led to power cuts and made the already feeble internet connection even less obliging. The name didn't ring a bell straightaway. Only when I went back to the message and noticed a PS, 'Are you still in touch with Mike?' did I recall meeting her a few years earlier through a mutual acquaintance in London and, although we got on at the time, and once later when we met for an exhibition at Tate Modern, we didn't maintain contact. Maya was a sculptor from Portugal and that was where she was staying when she contacted me. She wrote that she had recently come into a small inheritance that consisted of a disused warehouse in a village where she had grown up and was planning to turn it into a studio where she would live and work for most of the year. She had heard that I was in the area – hardly, Languedoc is quite a way from Portugal – and was wondering whether she could come and stay with me for a week or so.

The tone of the message was straightforward, matter-of-fact, without excessive niceties or unnecessary politeness, certainly lacking in the humility that one might expect from someone who was inviting themself to stay, in particular if that someone was neither a close friend nor a person whom one owed a favour. Or perhaps, I might add, someone who was in need of help or company which, I imagined, she was. Why else would she, whom I barely remembered, have invited herself to stay with me? Whatever it was, I found her dry tone reassuring. Any hint of sycophancy would have turned me against her. I was about to write back and ask her when she planned to arrive, but then another storm plunged us into darkness and I had to delay my response. In the quiet of the night, I was woken up by an owl hooting nearby and, while lying awake, I kept thinking about Maya's message. What motivated her desire to stay with me? How did she know my whereabouts? The more I thought about it, the more I became convinced that someone, one of my well-meaning but ever meddling friends, had put her up to it and that it wasn't her who was needy, rather one of the people who knew me, felt that I might be. A week after receiving the message, I decided that there was no point in carrying on speculating and that it was best to ask her to come clean before I committed myself to her visit. But as I sat down and switched on the computer, I realised that there was another message from Maya giving me the date of her arrival in three days' time. She wrote that she was sure I was looking forward to seeing her as much as she was excited about seeing me and that the reason she was arriving on that particular date was linked to her stay in Figueres in Catalonia. She was teaching a workshop to budding sculptors there and was going to take a bus the morning after the course finished. That made sense and somewhat dispelled my doubts: my house was probably less than two hours' drive from Figueres and she might have heard about my move to France and, without much deliberation, decided to visit me. After all, we had liked each other on those two occasions when we had met. There was also a separate message, sent minutes after the first, asking if I had a hair dryer in the house. That didn't surprise me. On each of the two occasions I had met her, she sported a different hair colour. I remembered looking out for a dark brunette and being accosted by a woman with green streaks. She laughed at my confusion and said that her friends never knew what to expect. Apparently, she changed her hair colour once a week. No wonder she was asking about a hair dryer. I looked around and located an old model in the bottom drawer of a linen cupboard.

I must say that I was not in any way anxious about her stay but nor did I look forward to it. After all, I hardly knew her; I had no idea what to expect. I was not craving human contact but, equally, the nature of my life style and the writing I was doing at the time – editing a finished novel – meant that I could accommodate a visitor without undue disruption to my daily routine. Besides, at that stage in my life, I had convinced myself that I should be open to new experiences, no matter how unexpected. You could say that my motto at the time was: *Que sera, sera.*

The day of Maya's arrival was also the day of the weekly market and, having picked up a good supply of fresh fruit and vegetables, I drove to the town, some thirty kilometres away, where the bus from Figueres was arriving. Since the market closed at midday, and Maya was due just before five o'clock, I had most of the afternoon to walk around. The town was small and within an hour I found myself in the same place where I had started. There were no museums, and apart from its elegant, but ubiquitous, nineteen-century residential architecture, mainly in the shape of stately *maisons de maître*, a park with a memorial to the victims of various wars, including the Algerian conflict, and a large *mairie* with a striking ochre façade, there was not much to see. As the weather had turned and it was drizzling, I thought of taking refuge in the *médiathèque* I had passed earlier but, when I returned, a note informed me it was closed on Wednesday afternoons. As the rain intensified, I had no choice but to find a café. The first two I entered were unappealing. Too crowded with locals shouting in French and Arabic. The relatively quiet one, where I finally settled, looked unprepossessing both from the outside and inside but at least I could sit in a corner with an espresso and kill the next few hours in the company of Ricardo Reyes' *Journeys Through My Mind: A Travelogue.* It was the first book I had come across by the great South American and even after a few pages I felt an affinity with his way of thinking. It was a hefty volume and I looked forward to immersing myself in its world.

Some of the surrounding tables were occupied and I couldn't help being aware of the other people. No one was excessively loud but a whisper here and there, or even their presence, was enough to nibble at my concentration. Three times I read the page with the narrator describing the extent of his ornithophobia. I scanned the text again and again but to no avail. Ha, the legacy of my grandfather. How could I mind? Any memory of him, old Joe, as his trade union friends used to call him, made me feel warm inside. On our long walks, we would randomly pick out someone we could see and amuse ourselves by making up stories about them. What was their name? How old were they? What did they do in life? What were they thinking about? Where were they going? There was no end to our questions. The only rule was to answer without thinking, coming out with the first idea that came to mind. Sometimes we ended up with fantastical creatures, doing jobs no one would have heard of, hailing from imagined, exotic countries. Grandfather considered it an excellent way of exercising one's creativity. If someone in the family made a disparaging comment about our activity, grandfather's response would be a quiet smile. But as soon as we were alone, he would say in his usual, conspiratorial tone, the tone, that I knew was reserved only for me, what he really thought: 'I don't need to tell you how boring they are,' and, saying that, he would close his eyes, drop his shoulders and with the fingers of his right hand mimic a series of imaginary letter Zs coming out of his head, all to demonstrate how sleepy our recently departed collocutor made him. 'Stories. They need stories.'

That was how we occupied ourselves on our daily walks for years before I started school and then later for the greater part of my holidays. Grandfather was an inveterate story-teller and my only and best baby-sitter. When I was in my teens, our narratives developed detailed, often cranky, characterisation and plot twists. The less we knew about a person, the more we could give flight to our imagination. Our stories did not meander in a random fashion. Anyone who listened carefully would have been able to perceive a pattern, even if invisible at first. A pattern. Internal logic. A figure in the carpet.

After his death, the habit helped me to deal with his absence as I alternated our voices to conjure new stories. I was never lonely. I could walk around and be engaged in endless conversations. By the time I was in my early twenties, I would have strained, had it mattered, to tell which of the characters that populated my head were born out of my imagination and which I had met in my daily existence.

My memories of my grandfather were interrupted by a woman who stood by my table and, more histrionically than was strictly necessary, took off her shaggy fur coat and shook it in front of her, splashing rain all around, rather like a dog emerging from a swim. A few drops landed on my trousered legs and I instinctively pulled my feet under my chair.

'I'm sorry,' she said as she stepped in front of me. 'Marie, my name is Marie.' She proffered her hand and I had no choice but to take it and give my name. She misheard it and I had to repeat it.

'Vanessa, what a deluge we are having. What's the world come to?' she said, taking a chair at my table. 'You don't mind, do you?'

A lie came out of my mouth involuntarily. My book was still open in front of me and I had hoped to give the impression that I was reading.

The woman smiled at me.

Lightning struck, illuminating the café.

'We didn't used to have such violent weather years ago,' the woman said. 'My husband says it's beneficial for the garden but what does it matter when we don't have one?'

With the rain bucketing down there was no chance of me leaving.

'Are you waiting for someone?' she said.

There didn't seem to be much point in avoiding conversation.

'Yes,' I said. I tried to give the impression that I was not interested in talking but that didn't bother her.

'I thought so,' she said. 'Everyone here is waiting for someone. A child to be born, a mother to die and leave them an inheritance, someone to answer their marriage proposal. What else is there but to wait? The whole world seems to be one large waiting room.'

I had nothing to say but that didn't seem to bother her.

'You see, I'm waiting for my son. I'm waiting for my son to graduate. An agricultural college. That's where he is. It may take a while. He is not an academic type. Most of his interests are terpsichorean. Always on tiptoes. That's him. But if it ever happens, if it ever happens that he graduates, then I will be waiting for him to find a job. Then I will be waiting for him to leave home. At that point, if it ever happens, which I'm beginning to doubt, I will stop waiting. I will take off. Yes, why not? I have no specific plans. No strong desire to visit particular places but I will go away anyway. After all, one goes away for oneself, not for the places that one visits. As for my husband, I doubt he would join me. Not that he hasn't been aware of my plans. God knows how many times I have spoken to him of my intentions and he has neither approved nor disapproved openly but that tells me that he is not interested in joining me. If he were, he would say so. He has always been a kind of man who tries to avoid conflict, which, you may think, is an admirable trait, but in fact, when you have to deal with someone like that, let alone when that is the person you live with, it can be somewhat irksome. With my husband, I never know where he stands. Even if he disagrees with me, really disapproves of what I'm suggesting, he wouldn't tell me. His speech is peppered with aposiopesis. But, over the years, I have developed a system where I observe the minutiae of his body language – not the face, mind you, he keeps that as straight as it can be – a slight tension here and there, a movement of the arm that is either too sudden or too large, a swing of a foot on a crossed-over leg, or his hand readjusting the wristband on his watch. In fact, that last one you would think is pretty innocuous, meaningless really, but no, you would be wrong. With him, it stands for annoyance, a touch of anger even. I had to learn to read him because, as I said, he is a man who hides his feelings. I know most men do, but my husband is probably worse than most, or better, depending on your point of view. He is a real master of covering up what he thinks and feels, and the basic rule I have discovered in reading him is to take it for granted that the stronger the feeling, the smaller the gesture he resorts to. You may think it paradoxical but if you knew how important it is for him to hide his feelings, you would understand that as being another twist, all designed to make him as impenetrable to me as possible. It may now seem obvious that a person who is keen not to reveal their feelings would choose such a system but, like all the best discoveries that seem obvious once they are worked out, I can assure you it took me years of observation, and careful observation, recording and analysing my notes, before I could arrive at it with some certainty.'

The woman paused to take a sip of her coffee.

The speed at which this monologue unfolded was spell-binding and I found myself watching her without thinking of what she was saying. Her words resembled a carefully rehearsed and often performed show.

'At this point, I realise I should give you some background on my husband and watches but before I do that, I must mention that my husband is a selenologist. That might explain lots of things about him. Anyway, when we first met and throughout our years of dating, he didn't have a wristwatch so I cannot tell whether he had always had that particular gesture, that particular way of covering his feelings, or whether he has developed it since he has been with me. Nor am I sure at what point he acquired a watch.'

She sighed, shook her head and took another sip of coffee. A waiter passed by. She asked him for a pot of olives and a glass of water.

'What I do remember is that one day as we were driving to see his parents for Sunday lunch, I noticed that he had a watch and I could not hide my surprise because he used to be a person who despised the idea of checking the time. Besides, for years he would dismiss the need for a watch, arguing that there were clocks everywhere, inside and outside – as you must have guessed, I am talking of years long ago, years before mobile phones with their own digital timepieces – and that therefore he was never in need of a watch on him. To give him his credit, he was never late. Or perhaps he made a point of never being late and might have been hanging around our appointed place for hours before the date, all to prove to me that watches were unnecessary.

'Anyway, I remember that day clearly because it was

pouring with rain and I had a bad cold and the last thing I wanted was to have lunch at his parents'. I must stress here that I did get on with them, oh, absolutely, like a house on fire; I really cannot say that they didn't welcome me to the family, they were people of enormous probity, even though one of their daughters, my husband has four sisters and it was only the oldest, she is dead now, cancer it was, breast cancer, yes, she tended to make snide remarks about my hair and clothes, always after she had inveigled me into her confidence, yes, that was part of her game but on that Sunday, she wasn't going to be present, so, really, I had nothing to worry about. That same person was often accused of presenteeism. But this is of no relevance now, you could say, and I would agree. What I am saying is that I wasn't feeling well; I even dozed off in the car, it was a longish drive and, as I woke up, the first thing I saw was that my husband was wearing a wristwatch. While I was asleep, he had stopped at a petrol station and had taken off his jacket, under which he had a short-sleeve shirt. That means that it was possible he had been wearing the watch before he stopped to fill up but it was equally possible that not only had he strapped it on at that point but even that he had bought it in the shop at a petrol station. It was a cheap-looking watch with a metal strap and the glass over the dial reflecting the light. Possibly, it was a brand-new watch. But when in my incredulity I exclaimed that he was wearing a watch, he leisurely dismissed it with a 'So what?' or words to that effect and added that most people wear watches. As if I didn't know it. What was the point of saying that? You see, that's when I became suspicious: a person who tells you the obvious clearly has something to hide. Not to mention his feigned equanimity at my surprise. Better beware, Marcelle, I said to myself. And I have been. I tell you, his readjusting the watch as a sign of his efforts to hide his feelings is not the only thing I have learned about him. I also think, well, not that I think but I know, I know that he is having an affair. I mean, I don't know as in know. He hasn't told me and I haven't seen him or any evidence, a note, a text message, anything like that, not that, but I have a very strong feeling that is the case. You know how we women have that sixth sense.'

Saying that, she winked at me and waited for my approval. Her eyes bore into me and I nodded in agreement.

'So, now you will understand why I am waiting, waiting to go away and why I am sure that my husband will not be interested in joining me.'

She paused and I nodded once again as, I could tell, she expected me to. My book was still open on the table in front of me and I kept lowering my eyes as if to give the impression that I wanted to read but the woman seemed oblivious to my efforts.

'But that's fine. I don't mind. There comes a time in people's lives when they have to take their own paths, regardless of what others may expect them to do. I can see you would agree with that.' She smiled.

Was that what I thought? I had no idea. I doubted I thought anything.

'Never mind,' she said with a shrug. 'I have a feeling you and I are on the same wavelength. Two women who have been through a lot. In relationships, I mean. Not that I regret it. If I had my youth back, I would do the same, go for the same man. It could have been worse. In fact if it were not for his reluctance to talk about our future, or at least to come out and tell me why he doesn't want to join me, you see, I could accept that, yes, I could accept that if only he were to tell me what he really thinks and wishes to do, yes, if it were not for his silence on this matter, I would venture to say that we have had a good marriage. Not perfect but then whose is perfect? Except for all this business with touching his wristwatch and then me having to read his signs, I tell you, that's not the right way to behave. Not between two people who live together.'

I expected her to look at me as she paused and I tried to think what I thought of what she had said so that I could oblige with a nod, but then her mobile rang and the woman began rummaging through her handbag. She seemed to have difficulty in locating the phone. Eventually she fished it out.

I repositioned my book on the table in front of me and tried to resume reading but her voice was much too loud.

'Oh, hello. Yes, I am fine, and you?' A pause. 'I know. Dreadful. Gale force. I had to stop at the café. My umbrella's broken. 'A sigh. 'Right. Okay. Could it not wait?' Her jaw dropped. 'What? Marcel? What are you saying to me?' Her forehead furrowed, her eyebrows jumped up. 'You can't be serious. Hang on, we need to talk about it. What do you mean there is nothing to talk about? You cannot simply spring a surprise on me like this. Why not? You're asking me why not? Because . . . because, I didn't expect you to go. It's been me who has been talking about it. And, what do you expect our baby to do? Of course he is a baby. Terpsichorean but a baby. He will always be a baby. Listen, don't go anywhere. I'm coming home. Listen, I'm still your wife.'

She stood up, grabbed her coat and without a backward glance rushed out into the storm. A waiter arrived with a plate of olives.

I picked up my book and read a couple of pages but could

not follow the text. Stories about people around me kept popping up in my head. I ordered another coffee, and as soon as it arrived, the sun came out and a rainbow arched over the horizon. The light dazzled across the glass tops of the tables. I finished the coffee and went out for another walk around the same streets as before the storm. Eventually, I made my way to the terminal; the arrival time of the bus was no more than half an hour away. A few people were already waiting. When the bus pulled up, only half a dozen passengers disembarked. I looked at each one of them closely, aware that Maya could have any hair colour, and soon realised that she wasn't among them. Perhaps she had missed the bus. The next one from Barcelona was in two days. I checked my phone. Nothing. I tried to ring her but calls failed, as if the number didn't exist. I sat down in the bus shelter, thinking what to do. All the others who had been waiting with me had left with whoever they had come to pick up. But one of the passengers, a man in a trilby and a ginger beard, was hanging around, walking up and down and checking his watch. He kept punching numbers on his mobile but didn't seem to be getting through. After several attempts, he put the phone back in the pocket of his jacket and looked up. I could see he was in his late fifties, with a fubsy frame. He spotted me and stepped in my direction.

'Hello, I'm Eric. You're not by any chance waiting for me?'

'I don't think so. I was expecting a woman.'

He laughed. 'Join the club. I was expecting a man to pick me up. At least that's what they told me. But when I saw you, I thought maybe something's happened and they had sent someone else.'

'Not me. I've certainly not been waiting for you.'

Even before he apologised for bothering me, I felt bad. I am not one of those people who is ever abrupt with anyone.

The sky clouded over and a fine drizzle pervaded the air. The daylight was fast disappearing. There was nothing to do but drive back home. I made my way to the car park. As I approached it, I looked for the keys but could not locate them in my bag. I poked the pockets of my jacket. After another unfruitful search through the bag, I emptied the contents onto the front booth. The keys were not there. The best I could think was to retrace my steps. That could have taken me a few hours. I thought I should try my luck and headed back to the café. The table I had occupied earlier in the afternoon was taken by a group of loud youngsters. I stood close by and perused the floor underneath. There they were, my car keys, pushed against a table leg. As I bent down to retrieve them, one of the young men, in a trilby and a ginger beard, realised what was happening and picked up the keys for me.

I thanked him and rushed to the car park. Driving in the dark has never been my forte but I had no choice. It was better to get back then to look for accommodation. On the way out of the town, soon after I had crossed the bridge and was about to take the right side of the road that forked in front of me, the car stalled. I lifted the bonnet – people usually check the engine when the car doesn't start – but I could only stare in amazement at the giant entrails of the knotted pipes and valves. My only option was to keep trying switching the engine on and, eventually, it shuddered into life, briefly, but sufficiently long for me to realise the car was out of petrol. Driving in at lunchtime, I had passed by a petrol station, probably a mile away from where I was parked. I contemplated what to do, whether to walk there and get a canister or to try to push the car. The former was probably more feasible. I locked the car and was about to set off when I noticed a man walking in my direction.

'Hello, I saw you at the bus terminal,' he said. 'You remember, I'm Eric.'

He stared at me and I don't know what made me say it but I told him that I had run out of petrol. He was walking to a guest house some five kilometres away and suggested that if I could give him a lift afterwards, he would be happy to get a canister of petrol for me. I didn't mind walking there myself but before I could say anything, he had asked me if I could open the car so that he would place his bag inside and set off straightaway.

'I may not look it,' he said 'but I am a fast walker. I'll be back in no time.'

Off he went and I got back in the car. He was as good as his word. Barely twenty minutes had passed before he appeared in front of me, canister in hand. We emptied it and on the way to his guest house, stopped by the petrol station and filled up.

I focused on driving along a very narrow road, more like a field track, and he didn't talk, except for reading out directions from a piece of paper he held in his hand. He directed me to pull up in front of what appeared to be an old sprawling farmhouse and Eric took his bag, thanked me and went to ring the bell. I had to drive on, up the track before I could find a space wide enough to turn round the car. A few minutes later, as I was driving past the house, Eric was still standing outside, the bag in his hand. He waved.

'There is no one here,' he said. 'It's empty. In fact, there is a note that the farm shop is closed for the annual holiday. And yet this is the place. I don't understand. I spoke to a woman this afternoon, on the very number that is on the note. I rang that same number now and all I got was a message about the annual holiday.'

'Hm.'

'Look, I am sorry, if you could take me as far as the end of this road, I mean to the point where you have to go in a different direction, I would walk from there and find somewhere to stay. It hasn't been a good day.'

'Okay.'

But when we got to the end of the road, I said that there was no point him looking for somewhere else to stay. I could offer him a room for the night. I had no idea why I said it, perhaps because I didn't care either way. He had a problem, not me.

He seemed to consider it for a minute before saying: 'I feel I've imposed myself. I really don't wish to take advantage of your kindness.'

That was silly. I wasn't being kind, only practical. I stopped the car and said: 'Look, you had better make up your mind. I don't wish to remain here on the side of the road. Not at this time. Either we carry on or you get out.'

'Thank you. I'd like to accept your offer.'

Again, we drove in silence, with me concentrating on the driving in the dark and with him, I don't know, probably thinking his own thoughts. In the house, we shared the dinner I had prepared in advance to welcome Maya and had a glass of wine each. I gave him a bale of sheets and towels and sent him off to the little annexe down the garden.

In the morning, I was up for half an hour and had finished my breakfast by the time he knocked on the French windows at the back of the house. I noticed that he had shaved his ginger beard. His hair – which I hadn't seen before since he hadn't taken off the trilby for the dinner – was black, jet black. He said he didn't want anything except for a cup of coffee. I showed him where I kept the groceries and went upstairs. I worked in the study until the early afternoon.

When I emerged, Eric was sitting in the garden on an old, rickety wooden bench, and sunbathing in the late October warmth. When he heard me approach, he took off his sunglasses and asked how I was.

It had not been a bad day. I managed to do more than I usually do and that always made me feel good.

'In fact,' I said, 'I am thinking of going for a walk, or a bike ride. You are welcome to come with me.'

'I can't ride a bike. But a walk would be good.'

We had a late lunch of a sandwich and an apple each before setting out.

'If we start off in the direction of north-west and carry on for three quarters of an hour, we will reach the canal and then we can make our way back on its southern bank eastwards,' I said.

Eric shrugged: 'As you say, I don't know the area and, besides, I'm not good with directions. North, south and the rest is all a mystery to me.'

As he had shown me the day before, he was a fast walker, but he quickly adjusted to my moderate pace. I asked no questions, but he seemed in a chatty mood and started telling me about himself. He was a northerner and it was his first trip to the Languedoc.

'I'm between jobs,' he said 'and when an ex-colleague, a friend of a friend, invited me to stay at her place, I don't know why but she did – in fact, it was her husband who was supposed to be collecting me yesterday – I thought I might just as well come down here as anywhere else.

'Normally, I'm very busy. Or, I used to be. Hardly times for holidays. Being here with no commitments, no tasks, no time to watch, feels a bit disorienting. It's certainly not something I'm used to.'

As we walked through a small village on the way back, he stopped at the square and pointed at the building to the left, whose side façade carried a painted image of a door and windows, around which stood several local people, casually chatting or going about their business. The detail was amusing: a journal half pushed into a mail box, as if stuck by the cover over the slot that had trapped it.

'I hate those things. Why do people think it's clever? Deceiving the eye? Hm.'

He was shaking his head. When he turned towards me, I shrugged. I had no problems with that or any other trompe l'oeil.

'What's the point of deceiving the eye? As if there wasn't enough deception. The world is full of liars.'

I let him talk. When I looked back on that first day of his stay, it crossed my mind that it hadn't occurred to either of us – he certainly didn't make any reference to it – that he was supposed to have left in the morning and looked for whoever his friends of friends were, whoever was meant to have been waiting for him on the previous afternoon.

In the evening, he offered to make dinner. I was struck by how easy he found it to cook in an unfamiliar kitchen and how confident he seemed at using herbs and spices lying around. I asked him whether he had been on courses.

'Courses? What kind of courses?' He paused and stared at me.

'Cooking, food preparation. Have you had any training?'

He laughed. 'Is that what you think? Oh, well. In fact, you might say I had taken a course, several courses, self-taught courses, I should stress. You see, I was married, to tell the truth, I am still married to an opera singer and I used to accompany her, most of the time, on her assignments all over the world. Anywhere we went, she would only eat what I cooked. It may sound strange but she had a phobia of chefs, for no particular reason, I should add, but she was convinced that she would be poisoned, and by that I don't mean an occasional bout of food poisoning, a stomach bug, that everyone gets from time to time, no, she believed that someone was out there to bump her off in an undetectable manner, cook something for her that would gradually reduce the power of her voice and eventually kill her. At first I thought she was joking but the more I came to know the world of opera singers, a very competitive world, glamorous on the outside but, inside, you sensed the knives were out. And so I realised that she might have a point and that it made sense that I cooked for her. She could trust me.

'At first, I was an average cook but as we travelled and preparing meals for my wife became my main occupation, I started taking interest in what to offer. There were days when she was physically exhausted with rehearsals, and needed food that would give her strength, at other times her vocal cords were sore or delicate with too much strain and I would seek out soothing ingredients. And she could eat. Physically, and in every other sense, you might say, opera singing is a demanding job. You cannot imagine the stress of maintaining a high-powered career on the go, living in rented accommodation . . .

oh, there were days and weeks when she was low, sometimes because she didn't get a particular part, was overlooked by a conductor, at other times she would complain that she was fed up with travel, too much work . . . there was always something. You would never had thought, if you saw her when she took a bow in front of the ecstatic audience, that she would be in tears an hour later, ready to chuck it all in. There was I, waiting in the wings, as it were, with her comfort condiments, scrumptious starters, delectable desserts. You could say, I was her personal chef. She sang. I cooked. We got on. I loved her singing. She loved my cooking. I took pleasure in providing ever more exquisite dishes. Mind you, it was not only her, there was her PR, cum secretary, her voice coach, her personal shopper, her hairdresser, her manicurist, her pedicurist, the driver, her personal trainer, image adviser, her beautician, all of them were happy to consume whatever she demanded. She was my main customer, of course. The more she loved my food, the more I tried. For my part, I can say that I tried to make my dishes varied for her sake and my sake. Cooking on a daily basis can be boring. I made sure I used local ingredients, adapted local flavours to her palate and needs. Those were the days.'

He paused and looked down. We had finished our meal and the two bottles of wine on the table between us were almost empty. I had had one glass.

After a few moments of silence, he looked at me and said:

'But I was useful in other ways too. Dying her hair, for example. In hotel sinks. Yes, in hotel sinks. That wasn't very glamorous, I grant you, but that's how she was. She hated wigs and preferred to have her hair dyed and styled as required for a role. Her hairdresser would cut and blow dry, but wasn't allowed to put the colour in. She let make-up artists do whatever they needed, including face massage, deep cleansing. No problems there. How many times have I watched the whirlpools of coloured water spiralling down a sink plughole? I cannot stand by a sink these days without thinking of my wife, stooped next to me, her head bent into the porcelain bowl, wet locks spread. Which reminds me, by the way, the shower in the annexe has an old, dirty curtain, one of those old plastic things that stick to your body. Slashed in places, probably worn with age. It gives me the creeps. I hope you won't mind if I take it down.'

I nodded to let him know it was fine by me.

'Good. I will do that tonight. Now, to get back to my wife, are you not going to ask me where she is now? What's happened to our fifteen-year-old idyll played out across the globe, in apartments and hotels close to major opera houses? The high life, people call it when I tell them my story. The high life that I used to lead. What's happened to put an end to our sybaritic life style? Aren't you curious?'

I didn't mind him telling me but I wouldn't have said I was curious. What difference would it have made to me to know about his past life?

'So, what happened?' I said to make the evening simpler for both of us.

'I knew you were going to ask. Everyone does.' The satisfaction in his laughter was palpable. 'I could tell you were a curious person.'

I opened my mouth, instinctively feeling I should deny his assumption, but he put his hand out and said, 'No, don't worry, nothing wrong with that. No, really, quite the contrary. I really don't mind telling you.'

I am not of the protesting kind. I never mind what people make of me, easier to let them get on with whatever they wish to think.

'Yes, I'll tell you, I'll tell you since you want to know. If memory serves me right, it was after one of those occasions when she felt hard done to by a famous maestro, one of those people who can be difficult to work with and who prefer to bring their own stars with them. It was the time of *Aida*, the casting of Aida, but my wife was offered Amneris, not the title part. It was mad, everyone could see that. She was a soprano, not a mezzo. Of course, she had to turn it down. At first she didn't seem to mind. I kept telling her other offers would come. The agent said the same, suggested a holiday. She wouldn't hear of it. Kept telling us she was fine. For a while, I even believed her, or rather, I wanted to believe her, yes, that's more likely, you see, when you know someone like I knew my wife, you cannot be fooled easily by their protestations. But we all hope, we all try to be optimistic and so I tried to tell myself that everything was fine. Nevertheless, I made sure all her comfort favourites were on the menu. It was autumn and the chestnut ragout with double-baked polenta was a tried and tested recipe; in the past it never failed to lift her gloom. As I was saying, she didn't seem put out in any way but I thought, just in case, just in case there is a germ of the slightest despondency, let me nip it in the bud. So, chestnut ragout it was. Jellies and rice soufflés, boiled pastries, all based on recipes that reminded her of her childhood. Yes, that was another thing with her: the constant foray into childhood. Whenever something didn't work as she had expected it to, she would want to read a book she had read as a child – *Alice in Wonderland* was always with us, I don't know how many copies travelled in our luggage, and Robinson Crusoe was another one – and of course, the food. Her childhood food.

'But, for whatever reason, the food didn't keep her well. Or maybe it did. It's possible to imagine that without it she might have become much worse. I will be never be able to tell. What happened is that she became more excitable, a jumpy bundle of nerves. Other offers came in. Violetta in *La Traviata*. Can you imagine? The role she had dreamed of for years. They pleaded with her. They were prepared to reschedule their season and all that to get her. No. A firm no. She wouldn't talk to the agent but to me she intimated that she was convinced Aida was to be the bellwether of her future career and without that she couldn't sing any more. I said it was only a matter of time before she was offered an Aida. No. It was too late. She had wanted the one from six months earlier. I carried on cooking, more and more desperately believing that my recipes would restore her back to her usual self, reintegrate what had fallen apart. But there is only so much you can do. The agent once again urged her to take a holiday. No. She didn't need a holiday. No, no and no. Everything we suggested was met with a no.'

The man closed his eyes and rubbed his face with both hands, before looking at me: 'Her cupidity took over our lives. Her cupidity. That's what it was.'

He sighed. The bottles in front of us were empty and I said he could open another one for himself. I didn't feel like having any more. But when he offered to pour me a glass, I accepted.

'There were days when I thought it was best to forget her problem and carry on as if there was nothing amiss. But I couldn't. I simply couldn't. I am not one of those people who can shelve the present, no matter how painful it is.

'And there was another thing: she who had loved cold weather, for whom the North Pole was a cryophilic nirvana, would shiver as soon as the room temperature dropped below twenty-five degrees. You might say that was the straw that broke the camel's back. I could no longer bear it. We were living in a sauna. Her assistants and I were sweating like pigs.'

He took a sip of wine, placed the glass in front of him and looked down. His face a gooey mellow. An onset of nostalgia. What a useless emotion. He lifted his head, his eyes peering into mine, and whispered: 'What do you think was going on?'

I had no idea. I said so. I had listened to his words but had let them pass without dwelling on them. In any case, it was a preposterous question. How was I supposed to know? But at least he didn't insist on hearing my view.

'Like you, I had not a clue. Eventually, after weeks of questions, she told me. She was in love. Can you believe it? She was in love. You see, I was used to my wife being infatuated easily. That wasn't a problem. Because of who she was, no one ever turned her down. But sex puts an end to infatuation, I knew that much. It kills the fantasy. She had affairs, so what? I never understood the importance people attach to that. Lovers come and go but husbands, let alone husbands cum chefs, they endure. Besides, she worked hard, she had to play hard. I would have been the last person to deny her that pleasure. It would have been perverse, selfish. Her affairs never interfered with our life together.

'But this was something new. She was in love. Or at least that is what she said. Not something like, I have a crush on, the words she had often used before, in the days when I had hardly paid attention to whichever name followed. But now she was in love! Imagine! I almost laughed. Not that I didn't care. And of course, I had my suspicions. Conductors. Casting directors. Star designers. Fellow singers. A fan. And then another surprise: she confided in me, in tears almost, that the man concerned had showed no interest in her. No interest? That wasn't possible. She must have got the wrong impression. Has she made it clear how she felt, I asked. Yes and no. She couldn't be sure. Why not make it clear? Because she feared rejection. She feared rejection! No. She who had never been rejected before. What was going on? I made suggestions, offered to send an anonymous message, go and see him myself, have his colleagues, acquaintances, drop a hint or two. No. She knew it wouldn't work. He didn't want her.

'Her life came to a halt. She wouldn't get up in the morning, she wouldn't see anyone, not even her PA – in fact I was the only person allowed to enter the room – she wouldn't take calls, even refused to let us pass messages to her. Something had to be done.

'I went to see the man. He was a carpenter in an opera house, the last she had worked in, for six months before she had gone kerflooey. Part of a team of craftsmen building the set and making props. A younger man, probably in his early forties. Mick, he was called. Even the name, the casualness of the shortened version, suggested he wasn't to be taken seriously. A rugged face, moustache, very thin. I couldn't believe my eyes. She had always liked tall, strong-looking men; even that I could accept, but a moustache. She was allergic to facial hair. Or at least that is what she told me. I shaved meticulously twice a day and as you can see, I am not what one would call hirsute. It couldn't be him. He had one of those twirly jobs, complete, I would imagine, with an ample daily helping of wax. I wondered if she had taken a good look at him. But that wasn't the time to explain, to rationalise her attraction. It was the time to act. And so I did. Talking to a few of his mates, I learned that he used to specialise in dining chairs, exquisitely made with no glue or nails, simply employing an elaborate wedging technique. But he had given up his business, which, apparently had been doing very well, when he took the job at the opera. They couldn't tell me why. In fact, he was a quiet man who kept to himself. No one knew anything about his life outside the workshop. But they all stressed what a fabulous carpenter he was. An excellent team player. A hard worker. I hatched a plan.

'Oh yes, I know what you are thinking. Yes, I did have qualms about going behind my wife's back. But sometimes, you may have been in such situations yourself, sometimes, we have to do things we don't approve of. The end justifies the means; that's what I kept telling myself.

'I went to see the man. I had already dropped him a note and asked to speak to him. We met in the theatre bar. It was in the evening and I thought we could talk over a beer but, no, the man was teetotal – what a pain – and all he would order was a glass of mineral water. He struck me as the incarnation of jejune. I got the impression that his hebetude knew no bounds. I told him who I was married to but I detected no sense of recognition on his face at the mention of my wife's name. That was new to me. I was used to people's jaws dropping in awe. Anyway, I said I was planning a surprise present for my wife: a set of dining chairs. Before I could finish, he stopped me from going further. He no longer did that kind of work. It didn't interest him. He was employed by the opera. I said the pay would be anything but nugatory; I could afford whatever he asked for and above. He wasn't interested

In money. The opera job was sufficient for his means. Was there nothing that could change his mind? Everyone had a price, I used to think. No. It wasn't a question of changing his mind. He no longer did that sort of work, he said. That was all. My plan failed.

'Talking to him, it became clear to me that he had no idea of my wife's interest in him. I realised that he wasn't affecting ignorance or lack of admiration. He was barely aware of her name. He said he might have seen it on a notice board in the carpentry workshop backstage. I had always imagined that craftsmen, and indeed everyone backstage, were in that job because they had a passion for theatre and were interested in the perks that naturally come with it. How wrong I was. He didn't listen to music and had never seen an opera. We parted. My wife continued to deteriorate. I was beginning to lose hope that there was any way out. Her will had been thwarted and she couldn't function. Only a miracle could save her. But I didn't believe in miracles.

'I discussed the situation with the agent on a daily basis. Could we kidnap him, the agent suggested? No, my wife needed him to desire her freely. She would despise him if she realised he had been forced in any way. The agent thought that was a detail we could deal with. I dreamed of drugs, something like that potion in Shakespeare, the thing Puck administers. But I knew I was a fantasist, the idea preposterous. The agent suggested we employ an actor, a lookalike who would take on the role. No, that wouldn't work. My wife would see through the pretence.

'The agent was at the end of her tether. She threatened legal action for breach of contract. Called my wife a diva, a spoilt child. I tried to make her take into account the effect the rejection had had on my wife. I understood it. Her affairs were part of her quest, the quest for her own identity. Now that the quest was hindered, had come to a halt, she could not develop as a woman, as an artist, she could not sing. She wasn't doing her work for money. The agent couldn't comprehend that. You see, they live in a commercial world, art is nothing but a product. I believed my wife when she told me that for women, sex was about knowledge and self-knowledge in particular. You could say that the situation, this new situation, offered plenty of opportunity for self-knowledge. I tried to point that out, but I wasn't sure I believed it myself. We had reached an impasse. Impasse puts a stop to development, kills opportunities, impasse means paralysis. Nothing to be done.

'Nevertheless, I carried on cooking even though she never touched anything I prepared. I spoke to doctors, therapists. She refused to see anyone. And then one day, I returned home after my midday bicycle ride and there she was, dressed, hair all done up as if she were going somewhere special, a clinquant butterfly holding her tresses. I had never seen it before. It wasn't the kind of thing she would have worn. She was sitting in her study and reading through the day's mail. When she saw me – I tried my best to hide my surprise at seeing her like that – she spoke as if the previous few months had never happened. I wondered whether the carpenter had contacted her and they had reached some kind of resolution. Had he given her the cheap hair grip? I dared not ask lest I brought back her previous state of mind. At her suggestion, we ate out that evening. Throughout the meal, I dared not hope that her problem had been resolved. We were not back to normal, because, if I can remind you, her normal included the fear that someone might try to poison her. However, that night, nothing could be further from her mind. She ate with gusto, platefuls of exotic, spicy dishes, the kind of cuisine she wouldn't have touched before. I had never seen her with such an appetite, not even after long and exhausting rehearsals. I complied with anything she wanted. And held my breath. And held my breath.

'I didn't have to hold it for long. The next morning I went out for my daily jog and when I returned, a note was waiting for me. My name was scrawled in her big loopy letters on an envelope that was propped up by a small candlestick on our breakfast table. I ripped it open. I read a neatly typed short note. She wrote she had to start anew as she had found the nimiety of emotions in carrying on with the same life too oppressive. I had been part of the life she was fleeing from and she had to make a clean break, abandon everything and everyone, even those she loved, like me.'

The man paused and looked into the distance. His face tensed and I could see that he was fighting tears.

'The strangest thing was that I wasn't shocked. But don't imagine that I had expected her to walk out of my life, let alone to give up her career. Also, I was under instructions from her lawyer not to try to contact her. That was two years ago and since then I have heard nothing about her. I have no idea where she lives, what she does, if anything, or who she lives with. Or if she lives.'

He filled up our glasses and forced a smile.

'An incredible story, my wife's, don't you think?'

'Yes, an incredible story.' It seemed easier to agree even though I had no view on what he had told me.

We finished the wine in silence and retired to our respective bedrooms, mine upstairs, his in the annexe at the end of the garden. The next day I worked until late. The weather had turned unusually inclement and a storm raged the whole day. I heard my guest below in the kitchen moving about and the smells reaching me in the study left me in no doubt that he was hard at work preparing dinner.

At eight o'clock exactly I was about to save my work of the day, when I heard him ringing a bell, an old iron bell that was fixed above the back entrance to the kitchen.

'Food is on the table,' he called.

I went down and the food was indeed on the table. At first we ate in silence, which suited me well, but towards the end of the main course, he said:

'When the lawyer contacted me, immediately after my wife had left, I was told that she had no hard feelings towards me, quite the contrary, but that it was best to get a divorce so that I could be free to pursue my own life. She wanted to stress, the lawyer wrote, that her marital status was of no relevance to her but she was concerned that remaining married might be a problem for me. When I protested I had no plans or wishes for another relationship, the lawyer made it clear that what I was saying was of no consequence. My wife had started a divorce and she was to have it finalised. That was that. I was to be given a generous settlement, far too generous for my lifestyle these days. The money has been deposited in my account but no divorce papers have arrived. As far as I know, we are still married.

'When I tell people, they think I'm a lucky bugger. Start another life, travel, get yourself a woman, or even better, women. They don't understand that to me one woman is like another. And there is only one I wanted. Only one I miss.

'But enough of my story. What about you?' he crossed his arms on his chest and leaned back in his chair.'

'What about me?'

'What is your story?' He was looking at me, his face serene.

'I write stories. That's my story. That's all.'

He stared at me. His face a question mark.

'Nothing more to say.'

'Nothing more to say?' He raised his eyebrows and kept them in place.

I thought I would have to make up some story about my life but, to my relief, the eyebrows went down and he asked no further. We spent the rest of the evening reading quietly in our respective armchairs.

The next day the weather continued in the same inclement fashion except that the rain was replaced by a wind that made the house tremble. I carried on working upstairs in my study, under the eaves, unconcerned by the racket from the outside, until the man rang the bell and called that the food was on the table.

He served a thick chard soup and we ate in silence. My mind was still occupied with the world of the novel I had been editing. Halfway through the main course – I forgot what it was, probably something with lentils, oh yes, it was a spicy lentil bake – he said:

'I do get lonely sometimes.'

I nodded.

'You do too, don't you?' he asked.

I shrugged. I wasn't sure. Being lonely wasn't something I ever thought about.

'Most people are ashamed to admit it.'

That wasn't the case with me.

'You must be lonely living here on your own.'

But I wasn't on my own. I had my stories. More stories than I could cope with. And now he was there. He with his own stories.

We finished the main dish and he served a fruit salad. As he was collecting the plates from the table, he said:

'I've been meeting women recently. Not that I need anyone. In any case, it wasn't dating. It happened. You get lonely at night and play around with the computer. Everyone does it. I chat to people. I don't meet just anyone. I try to be selective. But it's always something, something that bothers me. A kind of aggression. Violence. I don't know why that is the case. I wonder whether it is something to do with the expectations people have from those sites. The anonymity. The ability to project whichever identity you choose. Or maybe something to do with their vulnerability, lack of confidence even. Or could it be that it was purely a coincidence that most, if not all, of the women I met behaved in a strange fashion?

'Take the last one. We were writing for several weeks, sometimes several messages on the same night and I felt we came to know each other reasonably well. We tried to meet on a few occasions but she cancelled each time. She was a lawyer, married, but she claimed that was in name only. The two of them had been living separate lives. We decided to meet in a park, go for a walk and see where we could take it from there. That was her idea and I had no problem with that. A walk in the park was more promising than a coffee. By promising, I mean that what your potential date suggests reveals a great deal about who they are and to me a walk in the park sounded promising. Serious without being heavy. The kind of thing you would do with a friend, a girlfriend, ordinary, nice. We also agreed that if we wanted to spend more time together that evening, we would have dinner. She would get a really good bottle of wine and I was to provide the food. The division had to do with her interest in oenology.

'We arranged to meet on a bench by the Serpentine. I imagine you know the place? Hyde Park, London.'

The question was rhetorical; he didn't pause for me to answer.

'It was drizzling when I got there but she was sitting on the bench as we had arranged. We took a little tour around the lake, but eventually the drizzle began to bother us and she suggested we retire to her car. She said she had the bottle of wine in the back and if I still wanted to pick up a take-away, we could get it on the way to her place. I hadn't expected that. Her husband was away and we could go to their large flat in Mayfair. I said that would be fine with me and she said she fancied a Chinese meal and she knew of a place where we could drive and she would wait in the car while I went in and got the food. There was a great deal of traffic and we moved slowly but I didn't mind and I had the impression that she didn't either. It took us an hour and a half through the slow-moving traffic to reach the take-away she had in mind but as she parked, we were deep in conversation and both of us seemed reluctant to interrupt it and so we remained sitting in the car for a while, maybe even an hour. Eventually, I got out and walked across the road. By that time, we had spent almost three hours in each other's company and I was surprised how comfortable I was with a total stranger. As I got out, she waved and rolled down the window. 'You know,' she said, and she used my name, 'you know, E,' she said, 'you're a pleasant surprise. A very pleasant surprise. You're much

nicer than the impression you gave in our correspondence.'
I thought that was lovely and told her that. I also said that I
liked her very much.

'With a spring in my step, I entered the take-away. They
were busy and I had to wait a few minutes before I could
be served. I ordered a generous selection of dishes – I had
no intention of skimping and was looking forward to the
evening with good food and interesting company. As I stood
in the queue, I kept thinking of her and felt a kind of certainty that I could get on with her. I was definitely attracted to her and the possibility of spending a night together
was exciting. It took another fifteen minutes or so before I
received the packages and could make my way back to the
car. I crossed the road and soon realised that the car with
the woman was not where it had been before I had entered
the shop. Perhaps she had had to re-park. I walked around,
which was not easy with four large paper bags full of steam-
ing dishes in foil boxes. I couldn't see the car anywhere. I
checked my mobile. There was nothing. Eventually, I rang
her number. She was switched off. I rang again and again
and left a message expressing my concern for her, convinced
that something had happened that had made her leave. After
a good hour walking around the place with my four bags full
of Chinese food, I made my way home. I tried her phone a
few times again. It was close to midnight when I took out the
food – it was cold by then – reheated most of it and sat down
to eat on my own. I opened a bottle of wine and worked my
way through all the food. To my surprise, I wasn't sick from
overeating. I wondered how that was possible. There had been
enough food for at least four people, and I am talking generous
portions.

'In the morning, I knew the woman had stood me up. I still do not understand how I couldn't have seen it while we were together. Why couldn't she have told me? Why send me to buy all that food and then make a getaway? You see, the older I get, the less I understand women. Can you enlighten me? What's your take on this story?'

He was smiling and looking at me. It was clear he wanted an answer. But I didn't have one. What could I have said? All that mattered was the story, not my view of it.

'So, tell me. What do you think?'

'Why does it matter to you to know what I think?' I said.

'Why does it matter to me to know what you think? What a question. Of course it does.' His face assumed a serious expression to the point of appearing annoyed with me. I detected a tension in his voice.

'Well, it's obvious, isn't it?'

What did he mean? It wasn't obvious to me.

He leaned forward, his arm stretched out, hands gesturing towards me.

I sat back in the chair, instinctively moving away from him. I wondered whether I should have said that it was late and that I was going to bed. But something held me back. It wasn't curiosity regarding what he would say or do next. It might have been fear, brought about by the recognition of aggression, even threat, in his voice.

He fixed eyes on me. 'Tell me. Now.'

I had to say something.

'The woman must have changed her mind,' I said.

'I know that. But why?'

'You don't know, you who had corresponded with her, who had met her, spent a few hours in her company. How am

I supposed to know? She may not know either. Spur of the moment probably, or most likely there was nothing behind her decision. Nothing that she was aware of. Often there is no rhyme or reason to how we react.'

He nodded. His face brightened up but the voice retained its hardness.

'No! There must be a link somewhere, a link between something that happened before I went to the take-away and her departure. There must be.'

I didn't wish to contradict him.

'You're right.'

'Tell you what,' he said. 'Why don't you think about it overnight?'

It was a good moment to say good night. He too stood up and made his way down the garden path.

Next day when I woke up, there was a note on the kitchen table. He needed a few things from the market and had gone shopping.

I tried to work but felt restless and found myself walking up and down making endless cups of tea. Around lunchtime, I gave up. By now the sun was shining and it seemed like a good opportunity to take a walk to a nearby village, some six kilometres away. I took a country road that was hardly used by anyone except vineyard workers. I walked briskly, keen to wake up my muscles from days of inactivity. In the village square, I sat outside one of the two cafes and ordered an espresso. I basked in the sunshine until the sun moved and my table was in the shade. I drank a glass of water and made my way back, this time using the route by the canal. I met a couple with a child and a few dog walkers. We greeted each other, as was the custom in these parts.

By the time I reached the cottage, the man was cooking in the kitchen.

He appeared cheerful, much more so than I had seen before.

'Tonight, we are celebrating,' he said. 'With a cake. I'm making my favourite. It may be your favourite too, for all I know.'

I didn't have a favourite cake. I didn't have a favourite anything.

'That's good,' I said only to say something.

'Don't you want to ask me what we are celebrating?'

I didn't care to know but I had to ask.

'Well, I won't reveal it all, not as yet, but let's say that I have been making enquiries about my wife and . . . and, it's . . . no. Another time. So, let's say we are celebrating a nice day, a nice day after all that rain we've had recently. Isn't that a good reason to celebrate?'

'It most certainly is,' I said.

I offered to help with the dinner but he said he would rather I left him alone.

I went upstairs and read in my study. At the usual time, he rang the bell and called me.

He had prepared an ordinary, hearty main course, the kind of dish people in the region ate regularly, with beans, potatoes and cabbage.

For dessert, we had a *gâteau opéra*, perfectly executed with razor-sharp edges and a chocolate glazing that shone like a newly polished mirror. He served me a slice, revealing five layers of delicate almond sponge, flavoured with coffee and held together with mouth-melting chocolate ganache.

It was good and I said so.

'*Opéras*, how many have I made in my life? I've lost count. As you must have guessed, I was required to make it after every major show.'

Why should I have guessed it?

'I'm not surprised,' I said, conscious that if I didn't, he might ask again. 'It's delicious,' I added.

'Not that she would eat it. At most, she would have had one bite, literally one tiny morsel, but the cake had to be there. For luck. For her future luck.' His voice trailed into melancholy.

'Argh, what am I going on about? Boring you like this. How about a film?'

'A film?'

'There is that shelf of DVDs under the console over there. Look, let's pick something. Right.' He took a coin out of his pocket. 'There, heads, you choose. Tails, it's my choice.'

I nodded.

He threw a coin up and it landed on the table top. Tails.

'Better luck next time.' He shrugged with a smile.

He strode towards the DVD shelf and looked through the row of boxes.

'There,' he said. 'Are you sitting comfortably?'

I pushed the armchair from a corner to a place from where I had a clear view of the television screen. He handed me a glass of wine, switched the DVD on, slipped in the disk and settled on the sofa. His glass was on the floor next to his feet.

'It's been years since I've last seen it. I hope it doesn't disappoint this time,' he said as the title appeared on the screen. *Psycho.*

I hadn't seen the film for many years and, like him, wondered whether it would live up to the reputation it had in my memory.

When Janet Leigh finished rinsing her newly dyed hair and the black water rushed down the sink plughole, the man started hitting the side of his crossed leg and laughed. I pretended I hadn't noticed his reaction.

We watched in silence for a while but as Anthony Perkins started stabbing Leigh in the shower, the man stopped the tape.

'I'm sorry but I feel extremely tired. If you don't mind, I will retire. Do you want to carry on alone or we could continue tomorrow night?'

I didn't care either way. 'It's late. I'll go up,' I said.

The next morning I was woken up by a series of text messages, all from Maya. The earlier ones announced her imminent arrival, with no mention of why she hadn't come on the original day, now some three weeks before, and the later ones saying that she had been delayed and not to expect her for a few days.

I went downstairs and put a croissant – from a bag I kept in the fridge – in the oven to warm and made a coffee. The man from the annexe wasn't around. I finished the croissant and poured a second cup of coffee to take upstairs when I noticed a scrap of paper with a handwritten note.

'I've gone to town to get a new shower curtain for the annexe. See you tonight, Eric.'

I worked in the study until early afternoon. I was pleased with my progress and, with the sun shining as brightly as it does only in the Languedoc, I decided to treat myself to a walk. Passing through the garden, I noticed that both bicycles and the car were there. The man must had gone on foot to the nearby village from where he could have caught the bus, which passed through once a week. As I carried on the path to the village, I thought I might meet him.

I returned to the house around six o'clock. There was no sign of the man and I assumed that he was in the annexe. When he didn't turn up for dinner, I thought that he might have decided to stay in town overnight. Or perhaps he was tired and didn't wish to be disturbed. I value my privacy and have respect for other people's. That is why I didn't check the annexe for several days. When I did go in – I had a spare key but at first I knocked and then tried the door; it was left unlocked – there was no trace of him or his possessions. The shower curtain was missing and the sink needed cleaning. Black splodges stained the porcelain around the plug hole. I ran the water and with a bit of scrubbing, they came off easily.

I stayed in the cottage for a year and a half but had no other visitors. I finished editing the novel and wrote a collection of first-person-narrator short stories. I never heard from Maya.

The Bear and the Box

'THERE IS NOTHING I would like but the bear,' she told her husband.

'What bear?'

'A toy, it was his toy when he was little; a bear, a large bear standing on four legs, with wheels.'

He stared at her. Her father had been found dead a few hours earlier. That was the purpose of the phone call from her brother. From her brother in another country, the country of her birth. Her father had died unexpectedly. But what is unexpected about death? And what is unexpected about death at eighty-six?

After the funeral, in her brother's car, with her husband and her brother's wife sitting in the back, they drive past her father's flat and she thinks of the bear, her father's childhood bear, standing on its four feet, mounted on wheels, alone in the flat. She remembers how, as a child, she was more intrigued by the hole in the bear's side, where the straw stuffing leaked out, than by the object itself. 'When daddy was a little boy, he poked it to see what was inside,' her mother had told her. That bear is all she would like now that both of their parents are dead. But she does not want to go in. That would be indecent. Her father lies in a coffin in the queue to be cremated.

※

Days or weeks later she writes to her brother and asks to have the bear. She phrases her request tentatively, shyly, in case he might want the bear for himself or has already taken it.

'There is no bear,' he writes back. 'There has been no bear for years. Dad must have thrown it out. Eaten by moths.'

Oh.

Would she like anything else? She wonders but her brother does not ask. Yes, she would. There was a box, a wooden box, her father's mother's box, her grandmother's. She remembers her grandmother keeping money in it, house-keeping money in the days before cheques and credit cards. She remembers the days when she was a young child, her father borrowing money from his mother and she remembers seeing his mother, her grandmother, going to the wooden box.

If there is no bear, she would like the wooden box. Unless he wants it . . .

'Okay,' her brother writes back. 'I'll put the box aside for you.'

He Said Those Five Words

YOU DON'T NEED to go on asking me questions. I'll
tell you anything, without the prompts. I'm happy to
talk; I don't do much of it these days. And, as I said last time,
I don't mind you recording but I would prefer if you keep the
mike out of view. You're ready? So am I. It was at 6.55 in the
evening, on Sunday 13 November, that my husband walked
into the kitchen and opened a bottle of wine. He had just
finished a bath and I had cooked dinner. There was nothing
unusual in any of this for, in our late middle-age, and it is
right to say the same had been the case even in our youth, we
were people of habit. Not only had we learned to address our
insecurities, our fears of the future, near or distant, and our
fears of the immediate present, by relying on our set ways of
carrying out necessary tasks, but we also had become reliant
on the repetitions that maintained a sense of order in our
lives. To us, order meant comfort, order stood for security,
order made us feel we were in charge. And we liked that. I
came to think of those tasks, carried out in set ways, and
those orderly repetitions as our little rituals, and some of these
rituals I knew were peculiar to us as individuals, others we
had developed and shared as a couple, and there were a few
that we had adopted from society at large. We had rituals we
performed daily, we had rituals we performed weekly, we had
rituals that came once a year, such as those connected with
celebrations, and it was those annual ones especially that could

be tedious in their predictability, in their regularity, or at least that is how I began to think of them. When I speak of rituals I am not referring to the habitual actions that most people carry out on a regular basis, such as brushing their teeth at particular times of the day or catching the train at five to seven on workdays. Our rituals were the specific procedures that had become such an inalienable part of the way we lived so that their significance, their symbolic value, played a much greater role in our lives and in who we were, than the actual content of those rituals, the real action, the task – all of that we could have dispensed with if only we could have retained the symbolism. We had come to think of our rituals as givens, aspects of our life, indeed of the world in general, that couldn't be changed and that were going to be with us for ever. And it was the rituals, which I never doubted were required, which even I considered a necessity in our lives as individuals and a necessity in our life as a couple, it was those rituals that I had increasingly found tedious. My husband, however, had never complained to me about the predictability of our recurring actions, of our habitual tasks and events that took place at regular intervals, but even if he minded their predictability, I imagine he would not have talked to me about it, which in itself does not mean that he was happy with the predictability of our rituals, or indeed that he did not find them tedious, rather that, as I knew, he was not a person who tended to voice his discomfort. But unlike him, I have often found our rituals, and in particular those associated with specific times of the year, such as Christmas, or May bank holidays, irritating, precisely because they were so predictable, not just in themselves but also in the order in which they assailed upon us and sometimes I would wish, I would have a mad wish to do things differently, to have Christmas closely followed by Easter, with only a week between them or not to have either and then perhaps have a year with several Easters and Christmases, in order to subvert the expected, in order to subvert the norm, in order to subvert the necessity - although I knew that kind of subversion would be predictable in itself, unless - and that would not be impossible to arrange - the order changed every year. Was there no escape, I often asked myself, was there no escape from the rituals whose routine was grinding us down - or, at least, grinding me down - with its predictability, with its inexorability that moved like some machine that would never come to a halt, never run out of steam, like some terrifying *perpetuum mobile?* At times, I thought we were drowning in the quagmire of our repetitive tasks, I could see us imprisoned by the morass of regular actions, entangled, imprisoned even, by our set ways of living. If only someone or something could provide an escape, set us free, blow off the dust and let us breathe the fresh air. But that was a mad fantasy, one of those dreams that sustained me, one of those thoughts that gave me hope on days when things were not going well, made me think that there was a way of changing my life and even that I could bring about such change myself. But in the end, I was always too scared or perhaps too lazy to initiate any change. Or could it be that subconsciously I understood the power of and the necessity for our rituals?

Sometimes I would complain to my husband about him starting to look for, and then book, our summer French holiday immediately after Christmas or I would question why he ran his bath every Sunday at six o'clock. Why did he need a bath when having a shower was much more hygienic - I had only showers - and if he really liked having a bath, why didn't he have baths during the week or if he didn't have the time for a long soak on the days he worked, why didn't he have baths on Fridays and Saturdays? Why did he always have to have a bath on Sundays? Sometimes, a social occasion would come our way, such as an invitation for Sunday dinner or even for afternoon drinks, or I might have wanted to buy tickets for a concert or a theatre show on a Sunday evening and then my husband's first thought would be his bath. That was the time for his bath. How was he going to manage? Such concern on his part irritated me, not least because of the earnestness with which he spoke and it was more than earnestness in his voice, it was real anxiety at the prospect of missing his bath or, equally bad, possibly worse, having to have a bath on another day or earlier in the day on Sunday. I would worry about his inflexibility, about his intransigence, and in my mind I began to see him as a trivial person, yes, I mean trivial, for how could he seriously expect us to miss a concert – such as that time when I had booked a Bach concert for a Sunday evening and his reaction was not to ask what was on the programme, or who was playing the music, instead, he said, 'But what about my bath?' 'Bloody hell, I have booked Bach and you are talking about your bath,' I said. Wouldn't you understand that, sir? Or perhaps you're too young to appreciate Bach. But it wasn't only our cultural activities that were under threat; it was our entire social life. His need to have a bath on a Sunday evening, for it was a need, he experienced it as a need, I cannot deny that, this need meant that we had to turn down invitations to see friends, maybe even the invitation to share a meal with them – when such invitations were already few and far between – and all because of his bath. Couldn't he have his bath a bit earlier, couldn't he have his bath in the morning, could he not miss his bath altogether? But when I thought about it recently, I understood that his bath was important precisely because it was taken every Sunday evening and it would not have been important had it been taken on any other day but taken on Sundays over the period throughout his life, certainly all his adult life, the bath had taken on the form of a ritual that gave the meaning to his Sundays and not only to his Sundays but, together with other rituals he would have had, it gave meaning to his life. But not all of his rituals, not all of his habitual needs dated back to the beginning of his adulthood. Some were of a more recent standing, such as the ritual of our Friday night dinner, which he had initiated some ten years ago, out of consideration and, I like to think, in fact, I am sure, he had initiated it out of kindness to me, at the time when I worked full-time and after doing our weekly shopping on Friday evenings would come home later than usual and so he had the idea that we should have a convenience meal on that night, the idea that I welcomed, the idea that was practical and kind on his part, and that meal, brought about by convenience, always on a Friday night, stuck with us and we had to have it – for so my husband demanded – when I no longer worked full-time and did not have to do our weekly shopping on Friday evening and even when we were away from home on holidays, we still had to keep our Friday dinner. And although this particular ritual was a more recent creation, that didn't mean that my husband could be more flexible about observing it. After all, rituals are rituals precisely because they cannot be missed, altered or replaced by something else and the question of how old they are does not arise: once an event becomes a ritual, that is, habitual and meaningful to the extent that those involved think of it as being essential to who they are and to the way they see the world, that event is elevated to a status that makes it untouchable. More often than not, when I thought how sacrosanct his rituals had become to him, I wanted to diminish their importance, and so I had an urge to disrupt his rituals, even dispel them altogether, for I felt annoyed that an educated, rational man would care so much about such trivial aspects of our lives, such as not being able to have a shower rather than a bath on a Sunday evening and, when his insistence on those rituals interfered with other parts of our lives, I wanted to make it impossible for him to follow some of his rituals so that he would realise that without them neither the world nor he would come to an end. Thinking about it later, thinking about it coolly and rationally at the time when no tickets for Bach on a Sunday evening were booked, I knew that he knew neither the world nor he would come to an end if he had foregone one, two, three, or even more of his rituals, but that was not the point. That really was not the point. He knew and I had to accept that, had he foregone one, two, three, let alone more of his daily, weekly, or annual rituals, he would not have been in a life-or-death situation, at least it would not have been a matter of imminent death but I can imagine that the removal of a ritual, one, two, three or more, would gradually have the effect of eroding his identity, an effect that would not be immediately noticeable neither to him nor to anyone else but just as the addition of a grain of sand on a body lying down does not make a pile, before you know it, the body is covered, the body is buried under a large dune. And who is to tell at what point, at what critical point a few grains of sand become a pile or at what point missing one Sunday bath, two, three, four or more signals the end of the ritual? And who is to say that losing one ritual would not lead to the loss of another, until all of them disappeared and he, he as he saw himself, was gone too.

While I may not have shown complete consideration for his rituals on every single occasion, I was aware that his rituals, his obsessive desire to carry on performing them was part of the way he saw himself and, moreover, I understood that his need to observe his rituals was his way of defining his identity against mine. As a child, my husband had to have Sunday baths, and only Sunday baths, there could be no weekly baths, he had to wait for Sunday, since his family lived in a house with an outside toilet and no bathroom. This regular weekly ablution became an occasion, a laborious and time-consuming process that required heating up pots of water on a stove and pouring hot water into a tin bath placed in the middle of the kitchen and it must have been some kind of nostalgia for those early days, the days that had defined him, and created his need. By nostalgia I don't mean that my husband was sentimental about his childhood, or that he missed those days with the tin bath in the kitchen, and that he wanted them back, or that he hankered after the lack of privacy that having a wash in a tin bath in the kitchen neces- sarily entailed, but I could imagine that the ritual he had created out of that memory of the Sunday bath held attrac- tions for him that went far beyond the need for a regular soak. His memory, and memory is always selective, of those occa- sions in his parents' kitchen had allowed him to create a story in which he could make himself different from me and my family, from us who had never had to have a tin bath in the kitchen and who could have a shower or a bath on any day of the week. Now I can see that his idea for our Friday dinner, his idea to have convenience food, chips – I insisted on oven-baked chips, and although he had made it clear he would have preferred deep-fried chips, even he could see that oven-baked chips were much healthier than deep-fried chips – and ready-made vegetarian pies, the pies that despite being vegetarian and even vegan, reminded me too much of the meaty variety and that I could never have, I could see that his suggestion to introduce chips and pies to our weekly menu was his way of bringing back his childhood dinners, the kind of dinners that I had never had as a child with my family and the kind of dinners that he could use to distinguish himself from me. The fact that the Sunday bath could no longer serve its primary purpose of providing weekly ablutions in a household with two bathrooms and a shower room, just as the convenience dinner on Fridays, once I stopped working full-time, was no longer required did not matter since both activities had become ritualistic and had provided my husband with a place of safety, a place that allowed him to be himself. When I thought about his rituals in such terms, that is in terms of helping him assert himself against me, and I mean that in a positive sense, for I encouraged him to have his own identity, so when I thought about his rituals in such terms, I could understand his reluctance to give up his Sunday bath, I could understand his craving for chips and pies on Fridays. We ate chips and he had his vegetarian pies – the pies that I always found too meaty-looking and could never have but that aspect didn't bother my husband. (On one occasion in a supermarket he had even swallowed a few pieces of a meat sausage from a tray offered by one of those people who want you to taste a product and stand pushing their goodies in front of unsuspecting shoppers, and when I expressed my shock that he as a vegetarian ate meat, my husband claimed innocence, telling me that he had thought the sausage was vegetarian. I still do not know whether he was telling the truth.) The fact is that every Friday we ate chips and he had his meaty-looking vegetarian pies so that he could assert, if not forge, his identity. Yes, I do mean that. But the question was where did this need to see himself as different from me, where did it come from? We were different individuals, and while we necessarily shared a set of values – which was to be expected, after all what would two people be doing together, let alone be married to each other, if they didn't share certain values? – our views and our interests were anything but alike and no one who knew us would see us as too much alike, so much alike that we were indistinguishable, no, definitely not, there was no danger of that, and bearing all that in mind, I wondered why my husband had such a pronounced need, almost desperate need, in my eyes a needless need, yes, I mean a needless need – you think it doesn't make sense? – why had he such a needless need to emphasise the differences between us even further? I remember that my initial thoughts on this question centred around what I saw as his insecurity, but on days when I felt less kind towards him, the idea that a man in his fifties, a man who was professionally successful, and a man who had a family that cared about him, could be so immature and childish to focus on his insecurity, that idea irritated me. At the same time, I also worried that there was something about me, something that he saw in me that was suppressing his own development. Did I come across as too overbearing? Surely not. At other times, when I was happier with myself and therefore more inclined to be sympathetic towards the world in general, and my husband in particular, his insecurity almost endeared him to me and I thought that when a professionally successful man, a man with a family who cared about him, a man who was and therefore should have felt loved and cherished, a man well into his fifties, I thought that when such a man felt insecure, it was a sign of his sensitivity, of his vulnerability, both of which gave him extra points in my book. I liked the idea of being married to a man who was sensitive, and I liked the idea of being married to a man who saw himself as psychologically vulnerable. I liked that very much. But why couldn't he have talked to me about his problems, about his insecurities, about his vulnerability? Why couldn't two rational – I hope I am not overdoing it by calling us rational – two middle-aged people, living together, why couldn't they sit down and discuss their individual difficulties, their over-sensitivity, their vulnerabilities? What was the point of being together if we were not sitting down and talking through our individual problems, what was the point of being together if we couldn't do it? What was the point of being together if we had to hide our insecurities and invent spurious rituals? But if I am honest with myself, I did not raise that question at the time, that is, at no time before that Sunday evening in November did I think that we had not been talking to each other, let alone that there was no point in us being together. Of course we talked, of course we supported each other but those conversations were always about issues one of us might have had at work or something that happened in our relationship with a friend, little difficulties that we wanted to get off our chest, or ask for advice. But what else? Does anyone, does any couple talk about identity problems? You see, dear husband, or dear wife, I'm not sure who I am, but I can see that I'm not you, in fact, I think I could make myself

154

stronger by being more different from you and I can do that by introducing into our lives something from my childhood, something that you did not have, something that is only part of me and, you see, I want us to talk about it. No, we never did that. But who does? Do you, sir? Well, I am not assuming that you are married or the marrying type, look, this is just an academic question. A rhetorical question, as they say. I am not prying into your circumstances, sir. And there was another thing that crossed my mind months after that November Sunday evening: I wondered whether there was perhaps something about my own rituals, and therefore something about the image of my own identity that I projected on to my husband and that might have led my husband to feel the need to delineate his identity more clearly.

When I say that I had my own rituals, I mean that my husband would have seen some of my actions, some of the set ways of doing things that I insisted upon, he would have seen them as rituals. I, however, would have found the word derogatory, critical of me, in an indirect sort of way; you see, he always had a tendency to disapprove of some of my ways in a tentative, indirect fashion but would not say so openly. In my mind, there was nothing ritualistic about me washing the kitchen floor every morning, and sometimes in the evening as well, or doing ironing on a Friday night while at the same time we watched a DVD of a French film. I am sure you and everyone else would agree with that, sir. For me, until that Sunday evening in November, the activities that I performed on a regular basis existed only through their practical aspect. If I had to wash the kitchen floor every day and do the weekly ironing on Friday evenings, that was because the kitchen floor needed to be cleaned regularly and unless it was done every

day, and sometimes twice a day, crumbs, dust and various
debris from cooking accumulated and that rubbish was carried
all over the house. That was unacceptable; I could never abide
dirty floors. And Friday night was the perfect time for ironing
as it was the end of the working week and the day when we
could have a glass of wine with our dinner and relax. Too
tired at the end of the week for any serious work, reading or
learning, I was still keen to use my time productively. It made
me feel good to be able to tick off the agenda a domestic task
but, while engaged in this meaningless but necessary chore,
I also wished to have an opportunity to better myself. That
last requirement came in the shape of a contemporary French
film, so that all my Friday evening ironing sessions were done
while we watched a DVD of a film in French and therefore I
was improving my knowledge of the language I so much loved.
(My husband, however, chose to watch DVDs of sport or
recordings of old pop music concerts - hardly self-improving,
wouldn't you agree, sir?) And when it came to my insistence
that a chopping board, left out to dry behind the taps of
the kitchen sink, should be placed horizontally, that is, lying
on its longer side, rather than on its shorter side, there was
an obvious aesthetic consideration: positioning the chopping
board on its shorter side - all our chopping boards were rec-
tangular - would make it stand out as it would be jutting
above the bottom side of the window pane and thereby break
the straight line of the bottom of the window, I mean break it
in a visual sense, something that I always found disturbing;
however, positioning the chopping board on its longer side
allowed it to blend in with the bottom line of the window
pane and not to disturb the harmony of the vision. Isn't that
so, sir? My husband never had an eye for interior decor, for

visual arrangements, for the composition of a picture and, while I did not blame him for that shortcoming, I had to insist that he placed the chopping board in its right position. It was not a matter of a ritual, of repetition for repetition's sake. It was purely a question of aesthetics. It took him a long time to learn to do it correctly and even then I was not sure that he understood the necessity of doing it that way. What puzzled me about the chopping board situation was that, statistically, he had a fifty per cent chance of getting it right and yet, until I managed to get him to do it almost automatically in the right way, he would often, that is, in at least nine out of ten situations, get it wrong and leave the chopping board to drain lying on its shorter side. How was that possible, I used to wonder? I know I am raising my voice, but this is important, sir. Was the statistical anomaly a coincidence? I could not be sure and sometimes I suspected that he was deliberately refusing to position the chopping board in its proper way. That was bad and it would annoy me but I wouldn't have shown my true feelings, except sometimes, very occasionally, when I just had enough of his subversions. I suppose he saw my insistence as a ritual that had no meaning to him. But it was not a ritual. My ways were simply useful ways – I am a very practical, well-organised person – of dealing with necessary tasks in the house. I was a woman of substance and he was a man of form and symbols. Substance was essential – we couldn't have lived, I mean, we couldn't have lived properly. 'Proper' as in French 'propre'. Do you speak French, sir? But symbolism was optional, a luxury, an extra that we could tolerate when it didn't interfere with other aspects of our lives – as his Sunday bath did with our social and cultural lives – and that we should have been flexible about. I would point that out to him now and then and he would nod, sometimes even smile and add that there was one rule for me and another one for him. He was joking, I hope. Nevertheless, I should have given a more serious attention to what he was saying; I can see that now. But, as they say, sir, it's easy to be clever with hindsight. How couldn't he see the difference between decisions that were useful and practical, my decisions that utilised the time for domestic tasks to the utmost and decisions that were part of his need to draw a line between us, to create an image for himself of a person who did things differently from me? I was baffled. When I put it like this, I may be giving the impression that this question of our own rituals or, what in my case I had regarded as necessary tasks, was a contentious issue. That would be wrong. Despite our differences, despite my irritation with the tediousness of his rituals and despite my desire, my occasional desire to challenge his rituals, my husband and I lived in harmony. Absolute harmony, I assure you. If I may add here, my desire, the desire that I felt now and then, to make him take a more relaxed attitude about his rituals, that was more to do with my theoretical wish to introduce something new in our lives, to shake things up a bit, as they say, but by no means did I have any intention of subverting his identity. I knew that my wish to challenge my husband's rituals, for it was a mad wish, only a mad wish, one of those fantasies that some people, and I am one of them, like to indulge in while imagining that they are being daring. I knew that it was a mad wish because the predictability of my husband's rituals had become important to me; I relied on their predictability. I was reminded of that again when he said those five words.

When my husband opened that bottle of wine, most likely

a bottle of claret, for that was what we drank regularly in those days, certainly more often than any other wine – perhaps yet another one of our rituals – we were separated by a space of three metres and as I looked at him, at that point he was still holding the bottle in his left hand and a corkscrew in his right hand, I said that I didn't think we would be needing the wine. He turned towards me and raised his eyebrows. What did I mean? Had I cooked a dinner that would go better with beer – a curry perhaps? – or with cider, or would my dinner be best accompanied by something non-alcoholic? He wasn't smiling, but he didn't look anxious either. That tells me that my tone of voice must have been neutral, the tone of voice one would use to make a statement, rather than presage something unexpected. The expression on my husband's face was one of mild surprise but before he could ask why we wouldn't need the wine, I said something else. In time to come, I would look back on that evening and wonder what sort of premonition of what he was to say made me think, in fact made me know with such certainty – for I remember that there was something definite in my voice – that we would not be in the mood for wine and that our dinner would remain untouched until a few hours later one of us – I don't remember which one – threw it in the bin. I had not planned to utter those words about us not needing the wine because I had no inkling at all of what he was to say in response, and yet it was neither a chance utterance on my part, nor a habitual one. Could I have, sub-consciously even, been giving vent to my desire to undermine his ritual of opening that bottle of claret just before we were to sit down for our Sunday dinner? Thinking about it later, much later, I knew that my words came as a surprise to me as well and I could only conclude that they resulted from my unconscious feelings, or what some people might call my sixth sense, the intuition that women are supposed to possess. Are you nodding, sir? No, I didn't think you were but I imagine it's something you might agree with. You are the type, dare I say that, you're the type who thinks women have that special intuition. But if that were true, my female intuition would not have failed me so completely and left me with a total ignorance of the words my husband was to utter. But the question is, what was I doing saying that we wouldn't need the wine? And where did those words come from? Could they have been part of some destructive force in me? Remember, sometimes I felt like disrupting his rituals.

Just as I had not been aware that I would say that we wouldn't be needing the wine, neither had my husband planned to tell me what he ended up telling me. Yes, I am certain that neither at any time before or at the time of entering the kitchen nor at the time of opening the bottle of wine, had he any intention of telling me what he did tell me and, in fact, when I think of the casual manner with which he took that bottle of claret from the wine rack and the ordinary, well-practised way in which he proceeded to open the bottle, I am certain that nothing was further from his mind than the words that he did utter. Why am I so certain? Because he said it himself. And he added that despite not having any intention of telling me, he felt relief once he had said it. Yes, I do remember. His exact words were that he felt relieved of the burden he had been carrying on his own – which may well have been true. So, it was not just his nothing-out-of-the-ordinary manner that made me think that as much as I had no inkling whatsoever that the evening would not proceed in the most ordinary manner, in the same manner as hundreds of other Sundays we had spent together, that is, until the moment when those words that we would not need the wine came out of my mouth, until those words were said – I don't think I can claim conscious agency here – so, as much as I didn't know what was to come, neither did he have any notion that the evening would be completely different from all our other evenings. In months to come, as I thought more about his situation, I understood and came to accept his claim that the events he told me about that evening had never been on his mind when he was in my presence. The word that he had used to support his claim was *compartmentalisation*. Why do you ask whether I am sure of that? I swear, I am positive that was the case. I clearly remember him saying that men, unlike women, were good at compartmentalisation and the research I then went on to read seemed to support his claim. I would not wish to dispute that men tend to compartmentalise or that men act in a single-minded fashion and are better at focusing on one thing at a time, while women seem to excel at multi-tasking, but quite apart from this assertion being one of those offensive generalisations and, regardless of how many people one knows who conform to it, such assertions are bound to be untrue, as there are always individuals, and numerous ones at that, whose behaviour does not conform to the statement. Yes, sir, I feel strongly about this. I am someone who has always been suspicious of innate gender differences; I have a problem with the idea that men are somehow genetically *programmed* to compartmentalise, just as I have a problem with the idea of female intuition. When my husband talked of his tendency to compartmentalise, I believed that *he felt* his mind worked in such a way but it still does not mean that I could accept it, or that it was true that compartmentalising was the way his mind really worked, let alone was compelled to work. I don't understand, sir, why you're asking me to think about this. No, I didn't confuse it with our discussions before that Sunday in November. We never talked about compartmentalisation; in fact the word was never mentioned between us before that Sunday in November. And no, it's not someone else with whom I talked about compartmentalisation. What I wish to say is that whether his claim was true or not, whether it was credible to me or not, didn't really matter. Here was my husband, a man who had spent so much time and effort on forging his identity and this man was claiming that his mind operated in the same way as that of other men, as that of half the population. It was this recourse to the idea of compartmentalisation, this giving in on his part that puzzled me; that was the first thing that puzzled me but that was not the only one. In the months after that Sunday evening, it was my sense of disorientation, rather than this issue of compartmentalisation and its plausibility or not, that became the overwhelming matter in my life. I was lost. I was lost to myself. And he was lost to me.

But to get back to that moment in the kitchen at 6.55 on Sunday 13 November. When I heard those words, those five words that came to constitute his revelation, my body lost all sensation of its weight and of its corporeality and had anyone stuck a needle into my arm, or my leg, or indeed anywhere into my body, limbs or face, I would not have felt anything. The words that my husband spoke, that sentence, that sentence that contained no more than five words, anaesthetised me. At the same time, my mind was emptied of everything that it had ever known or been aware of. Once the words were spoken, my conscious awareness of myself and of anything around me was obliterated to the point where the world around me was taken out of existence. I was standing in the kitchen without knowing that I was I; I was in the kitchen without knowing where I was. When my awareness of myself started coming back, and I began to have some notion, some notion of who I was, it was my surroundings and the man in front of me who seemed unknown, unreal even. It felt as if someone had placed white gauze between me and the space around me, and this new world, this unknown world, a world in which I felt lost, this world appeared through a haze, like a dream. We were standing in a room that I had never seen and I had to screw up my eyes to try to find out where I was. The place looked like a kitchen, somebody's kitchen, somebody whom I didn't know and had never visited. I couldn't determine which colour and what material those worktops were made of; I tried to step nearer to see better, to touch the objects around me, but my legs wouldn't move. I tried to stretch my arms but they seemed locked in place. I could hear humming and I remember thinking that it sounded like a fridge but my ears wouldn't let me determine where the noise was coming from. With my body paralysed and my mind in a state of amnesia, I should have felt calm but I didn't. Something somewhere inside me was trying to get out. I wanted to move but I couldn't. I wanted to speak but I couldn't. And who could I have spoken to, anyway? A few metres in front of me stood a man who looked exactly like my husband and yet I knew, I was sure, he was not my husband. He was nothing like my husband. But why did he have the face shaped in the same way as that of my husband and why was his body built in exactly the same way as the body of my husband, and why did his voice sound exactly the same as that of my husband? And when this man spoke, all I could think was how dare he speak to me and speak to me in the tone that suggested familiarity, how dare he call me by my first name? How dare he? His words had nothing to do with me and I didn't want to have anything to do with him. But where was my husband? This man looking at me and saying things that had nothing to do with me, things that I didn't want to hear, things that didn't make sense, who the hell was he, this usurper, this thief, this intruder? Had he murdered my husband and assumed his identity? Take note of that, sir. That's what happened. That should be the line of your enquiry. I disliked that man and I wanted to make him go away. I wanted him to leave me alone but he stepped towards me and said my name. He was sorry. Sorry? What for? I didn't know him; I didn't want him to use my name. There was nothing to be sorry about. We were strangers who had never done anything together. Then came another sorry. And many more sorries. His sorries had nothing to do with me. And he called me by my name. And again. How dare he? I had to stop him. I wanted to scream, wanted to tell him to go away, I wanted to push him over. The bastard. More bloody sorry. And my name. My name. Stop it. Stop it. I wanted to shout but couldn't. The fool, the idiot – for what else could he be? – was sorry, sorry, sorry. He was sorry and then he said my name. My name. Again. I wanted to stop my ears. I wanted to cover them with both hands.

I understand. You are having problems with the machine, sir. I can wait and resume when you are ready.

Those five words? You have asked me that before, sir. You don't understand: the words were not important. It was the effect they had on me and the effect that that, in turn, had on him. There could have been other words, other very different words that could have brought about the same effect. The issue that bothered me after the confusion brought about by those words had gone, and after I realised what had thrown me, and I realised that soon afterwards, the issue was not what he had said, that was irrelevant, for things happen, things come and go but what stays is our understanding of them, or in my case, the lack of understanding. That's what mattered, wouldn't you agree? For it was the shock, yes, the shock of not knowing the other, the other who was my husband, my husband who was always predictable with his habits, with his set ways of doing things, with his rituals of Sunday evening baths and Friday dinner or chips and vegetarian pies, my husband who would never choose to wear a shirt chosen from his wardrobe at random but who would always put the set of eight or ten shirts from the previous week, the shirts that had been washed and ironed, he would always put them at the back of the rail in his wardrobe – no queue jumping, no preferences, no special privileges – so that they had to wait in the queue for their turn to be worn, my husband who was always so predictable so that you could work out which shirt he was going to wear on a particular day for weeks, if not months, to come, my husband who was so ordered, this husband did something that I could not have foreseen. I could never have expected him to use those words, the words that other people use, other men, I mean, but not him. And that is why I was standing there totally empty. I was asking the man, that man who looked like my husband but who was not my husband, I was asking him to stop saying he was sorry. He didn't listen to me. He went on saying he was sorry. I was asking him to stop saying my name. He didn't listen. He went on saying my name. I was asking the man to go away. He didn't listen but he did go away. And then I was alone. And it was quiet. Very quiet. Completely quiet. I liked that. I could think. I could think my thoughts. And then I started thinking about my husband. And I missed him. And I wanted to see him. I wished that. I asked someone to get my husband to come to see me. I asked again. But he never came back. And do you know why? He never came back because he was hurt that after twenty-five years of marriage, after twenty-five summer holidays in the south of France, after twenty-five Christmases, his wife did not know him and his wife could not tell that he would say those five words. And it served me right. I did feel shitty. What was the point of living with someone for a quarter of a century if on a Sunday evening, after a regular weekly bath you come to the kitchen and you open a bottle of claret, as you always do, and you say five words that your wife could never have imagined that you could say? What was the point? There was no point. You might just as well stay alone.

And that's the story, sir. That is the whole story. You can turn off your machine now. That's the whole story. I have not hidden anything from you. There is nothing more to say unless you want to hear what I do now. I do nothing now. I have no rituals. That is what I do. One should bring order to one's life. I have always been fond of order. True. But remember: sometimes I felt like disrupting his rituals. I know I will die here, amongst these walls.

Secrets

'HE DYED HIS hair, the old bugger,' my niece says. But his hair was grey, white, old person's hair.

'I found a silver bottle in his bathroom,' my niece says and shakes her head, her head of green locks. She sports a different colour every week. And yet she laughs at him, and yet she shakes her head at the memory of the silver bottle in her grandfather's bathroom.

I don't disapprove of my father dying his hair but I am taken aback, I am taken aback because I did not know. But why should I have known? Because he was eighty-six, and so I assumed, wrongly and stupidly, just like my niece did, that his life was simple and transparent to us, that his life was without sex or vanity, without secret purchases or desires. Within days of his death I unearth other surprises about my father's life. It makes me sad that I did not know him better, now that it is too late to find out more, but I am also pleased that he had a life I did not know about. I am pleased that he was more than an old man, every old man.

Part of that pleasure comes from the selfish thought that, despite my fear that in my old age I too will be seen by my daughters, and granddaughters – I can forgive the world at large – as an old person, no more than an old woman, when in fact, I would have had a private life beyond what they would have known and expected me to have.

I will keep my secrets and hope they will give joy to my daughters when they discover them after my death.

A Friendly Encounter

S HE SAID SHE had gone to meet her ex-lover in his flat. In the days when they saw each other regularly, they had the use of a pied-à-terre, lent to them by a friend who lived outside London. Out of courtesy or perhaps because her lover thought she would not know the way to his place, he picked her up from the station.

She had been abroad and they had not seen each other for more than five years. He said she looked well and, without having a real opinion about his looks – had the years ravaged him or not? – she returned the compliment. It wasn't difficult to be friendly and try to make her ex-lover feel at ease. He said they would have to take a detour as he wanted to pick up a newspaper on the way. She didn't mind. It gave her the chance to see the area.

He also said that when they arrived at his place, he had a small job to do, that is, a small job before they embarked on the possibility of restarting their physical relationship. They had spoken regularly on the phone for several weeks prior to this – what she called in a text message to him – 'a friendly encounter'. They seemed to have reached an understanding that since neither of them had a lover at the time, and both were missing sex, they might just as well 'be nice to each other'. Or did they talk about 'helping each other out'? She couldn't remember the exact words they had used.

On the way to the flat, her ex-lover talked a lot. She noted that he was more self-contained, and much less interested in her, than she had remembered. In the context of a friendly encounter, of helping each other out, that was fine. Or, he could have been nervous. She was a tad nervous too. More than a tad. But what was there to be nervous about? He wasn't Monsieur Landru. No, there was no danger from this man she had known for years. Could she have been nervous that he might find her boring? And perhaps he did. Perhaps that was why he talked so much. Perhaps that was why he didn't ask for her views on what he talked about; he simply presented his.

What did he talk about? He expanded his views on a philosophical concept, one of those she remembered as being his pet interest. He also referred to several relationships he had had since the two of them had split. One of them, which lasted longer than others, was with a woman 'who was not a writer or an artist' but she had said something 'very perceptive about her and me'. He quoted that 'memorable phrase' from the woman and asked her, his ex-lover, to whom he was talking now, for her opinion. 'Yes, it's an interesting phrase,' she said and she did mean it. Later on he would say that it was bad manners talking about past relationships to a possible new one (or even not the one so new). She agreed with that but this time it didn't feel rude as neither of them had any hopes or wishes, let alone desires, for more than 'a helping hand' between them and therefore felt no jealousy at all. In fact, she found hearing about his women intriguing. Who knew when she could use it in a story?

When they reached the house, he got on with his small job. He had already explained to her what he needed to do: ring the *mairie* in a small village in the south of France on behalf of a friend of his who did not speak French. That friend had been concerned about a couple who lived in the area, who were both in their mid-eighties and from whom he had not heard for three weeks despite calling them – he could hear the phone ringing at the other end and that increased his concern – and sending them emails. Her ex-lover had already spoken to the *mairie* earlier in the morning and they had agreed to send someone to check on the couple and now her ex-lover was on the phone and calling back the *mairie*, as he had been asked to. A woman at the *mairie* needed to be reminded by the ex-lover that he had already called and what he was calling about. Eventually, the woman said that the man to whom the ex-lover had spoken earlier was not around as he had already left. But when the ex-lover repeated that he had been asked to ring back in an hour, she asked him to wait. After a minute or two, the phone at the other end was picked up by the man to whom the ex-lover wanted to speak. That man told the ex-lover that he had been to see the couple and that they were in and well. There was no problem. He had informed them that an English friend of theirs was trying to get in touch with them and was concerned that something was not right. (That friend, just as the ex-lover, maybe even the man from the *mairie*, and certainly her, now listening to the telephone conversation between the ex-lover and the man in the *mairie*, all of them had already visualised the bodies of the old couple decomposing for weeks in their house.) But why had they not been in touch? 'Well,' the man from the *mairie* said, 'the couple's phone and their internet had been out of action for the past three weeks.'

She laughed loudly. Her ex-lover, still on the phone, looked up.

'Sorry, I couldn't help overhearing,' she said to her ex-lover.

'A happy ending,' he said once he had rung off.

'Yes, quite a story,' she said.

After that, her ex-lover rang the friend on whose behalf he had contacted the *mairie*, that is the friend of the couple, the friend who had been concerned about them, and the friend who did not speak French and therefore could not ring the *mairie* himself, and the ex-lover told him the good news, and then the small job could be put *ad acta* and the two of them, her and the ex-lover, could go to his bedroom and start their 'friendly encounter'.

But they didn't. Her ex-lover remained seated and carried on talking about the small job he had just accomplished. He appeared fascinated by the conclusion to his small job. She could see that the thought of retiring to his bedroom could not have been further from his mind. When she looked back on the time after the telephone conversation, she realised that at no point did the thought cross her mind either. Why was that? After all, she was in that flat with this man who used to be her ex-lover so that he could become her lover, her present lover. Instead, both she and her ex-lover carried on talking about the elderly couple in France and their worried friend somewhere in England. The happy ending was a relief for the friend and a good thing for the couple but as a closure to their own story, that of her and her ex-lover, it was a let-down.

'Or could it be,' she said, 'that the story provided a substance, content – or should I call it an event? – for our friendly encounter? A few days later,' she carried on, 'I began to wonder whether the couple whose phone and internet were not working and who had a friend concerned about their wellbeing existed or whether my ex-lover, of course in complicity with me, had enacted the two telephone conversations.

Shakespeare on the Buses

THAT QUESTION, THAT question is not asked as
often as it used to be, and here I am referring to the
words of Jean Gauthier, the inventor of modern autobiography,
V said to me when I came across her the other day in Parc
Monceau, through which I took a short cut on my morning
stroll. V was on her usual daily jog – typical of her, I thought,
this person who seems to be connected to the world in the
most fleeting of ways. I too, she said, have come to understand
the question is not asked so often because people are more
used to exiles, voluntary exiles like me, but it still happens
that they do ask, although not as often as they used to and that
is good, that in my opinion is a very good thing that people
ask less frequently whether I miss my country, and on such
occasions I still want to scream back at them, V said. To start
with, it is not my country that they are referring to, V said,
the country they are expecting me to miss, but it is only a
place where I was born and that does not make it my country
and those people asking that question ought to think what it
means to say that a place is someone's country. For, if there is
such a thing as one's country, one would have to identify with
whatever makes that country what it is (customs? National
football team? National dish?), one would have to feel at one
with its language (can any thinking person, let alone a writer,
ever feel at one with a language), one would have to be part
of its history (the history written by whom?), one would have

to feel at home with its traditions (ho, ho, can there be an agreement on those?), one would have to share its way of life (what is that? Drinking wine, drinking coffee, drinking tea?), but when I think about all of that, I realise that no two people would be in agreement. The whole issue arising from that question is so irrelevant, so meaningless that I am surprised that despite reading all of Thomas Bernhard, I cannot recall any instance where his narrators rail against it. Unless, and this is possible, despite my careful reading, I have missed it. Whether I am right or wrong on this point, and I do intend to go back to Bernhard and reread his entire oeuvre, people should stop repeating clichés about mother countries, father countries, sister countries, aunt countries, the clichés that they have heard from others, the clichés they have heard from their parents, that they have heard from their grandparents, the clichés they have heard from their great-grandparents and they should stop expecting me to answer using the same clichés I have heard from my parents and using the clichés I have heard from my grandparents and using the clichés I have heard from my great-grandparents. They should think about it and they should see that it is a matter of an accident of birth, of being born here or there, or nowhere or everywhere, that is a matter of being a wheeling and extravagant stranger of here and nowhere, to paraphrase Roderigo's description of Othello, the description that in his eyes is meant to denigrate the general in front of proud, nationalistic Venetians, but for me the words represent a compliment, hidden praise, and I can hear a touch of envy in the speaker's voice. Being born in a particular place is a matter of contingency and so why bother, why ask, why associate so much meaning to that place? As Luis Jose Salgado y Nuncia, the Uruguayan linguist, writes:

'People do not stop to think. Instead, they go on repeating words, they take language for granted and the words they utter are echoes of those they have already heard.' I am reminded of Robert Walser's comment, she said, that with our fellow humans the light goes out when they are born, and they spend their lives sitting and believing. Exiles, however, exiles of all types, those who are geographically displaced, or those who think of themselves as exiles, that is, those who lack a sense of belonging to their surroundings, those who live in different languages, tend to be more careful with words. In my view, what really matters, or used to matter when countries were different from one another, what used to matter, or should have mattered, she said, would have been the choice one made – assuming one could make such an open choice of which country to move to. That is something one could have a discussion about, that is something one could ask about and explain why one has chosen a particular place over all the others, what it is that one has been attracted to, what kind of myth one had harboured before one leapt, before one leapt into exile. As Günter Scholl, German scholar of nineteenth-century history, argues, 'That something that attracted the exile to the country to which one exiled oneself, that something is bound to have been a myth. Therefore the question is, what kind of myth it is that one has been attracted to, or even what kind of myth one has been repelled by in the country from which they exiled themselves.' Over the years, I too have come to think that those are valid questions, questions worth asking, V said.

When I think of such myths, of the myths that represented England for me, V said as we approached the path by the statue of Charles Gounod, there are many, many myths that attracted me to move to England but two are most powerful, by which I mean powerful in my memory and that, I have to stress, does not mean that they were the most powerful at the time when I leapt, when I chose England as the country to move to, as the country of my exile. Myth one, V said, and here I have to make sure to be clear that it was not necessarily the most powerful myth at the time, but it may have been and it certainly appears as such now that I am telling you a story of my life: myth number one was England as the country of Shakespeare. That myth of England as the country of Shakespeare, that myth was closely followed, and it is closely followed now, in my memory, by myth number two and that myth meant I took it for granted that the TV series *On the Buses* was an accurate representation of life in England. The juxtaposition of these two myths may strike someone as absurd, as utterly absurd, V said, and a friend, Sophia, who is a friend of many years, Sophia, who as you know, since you have met her several times, is a person of imagination, a person who has always led an unconventional life, she asked me the other day: 'How could you think something like that? Did you imagine Stan Butler playing Hamlet in between shifts, did you imagine him going to see a Shakespeare play accompanied by his mother, sister and brother-in-law?' Sophia said. V could not remember whether she ever thought of the two myths in such terms, but the fact that the two myths coexisted in her mind, coexisted without being linked, was not absurd and not only was it not absurd, it was indicative of something she came to understand later. These days, she can see that linking the myth of the England of Shakespeare and of the England of *On the Buses* is telling, is appropriately telling of class separation, of the typically English kind of class separation, the kind that she had not noticed as being equally pronounced in any other country she had visited, and in that sense perhaps, the juxtaposition of her two myths, of her two visions of England, two visions that she formed from afar, was perceptive, in fact, as perceptive as any other view about the country that she has formed since living there. But in the days when the two myths coexisted, or supposedly coexisted in my mind, V said, that is, if I can trust my memory, I was not aware of that division, of that social division.

On a day trip to Birmingham, where I was to attend an interview, an interview to be admitted to postgraduate study of Shakespeare, on that day I stepped off the train and asked the first person I saw the way to the Shakespeare Institute. That person was gobsmacked, that person had no idea how to respond to my request and as soon as that person recovered from hearing my question, he shook his head and walked off. Something was wrong with that person, I thought, something had to be wrong with him for he was in Birmingham where the world-famous department, or so I thought, the world famous department for the study of the greatest English writer, was based, so how could it be possible that he would not tell me which way to go. I even considered whether anything I had said, or the manner in which I had spoken, might have been off-putting, offensive, too much off the cuff for that person. It never crossed my mind that the person may not have known about the Shakespeare Institute, V said. The next person I stopped and asked the same question was more talkative than the first one and so the next person said she had never heard of the place and again I thought that something had to be wrong with that second, that more talkative, person, but when the same happened with the third person and the fourth person and the fifth person, I did not know what to think. Was it possible, was it possible that everyone I stopped in Birmingham had something wrong with them, what were the chances that everyone I had stopped had something wrong with them, something that made it impossible for them to be aware that the greatest English writer, who was born not far from the city, that the greatest English writer was being studied in their vicinity and by scholars of international repute and that they, these inhabitants of Birmingham, were not aware of that? Many years later it occurred to me, V said, that the people I had stopped in New Street in Birmingham to ask how to get to the Shakespeare Institute, that all those people would have come from the life represented in *On the Buses*, except that by the time I realised that, on the cusp of the ninth decade of the twentieth century, some things had changed and the world of Stan Butler, the world that was always a clichéd representation of working-class life, something that did not appear to me as such when I had first watched it, something I did not understand at the time when *On the Buses* stood for England in my mind, that world of Stan Butler, no longer existed. That world of Stan Butler, V said as we passed by a group of small, Parisian children, holding hands and walking in pairs while listening to their teacher about the history of Parc Monceau, that world of Stan Butler and his conductor friend had changed so much that the allegiance Stan Butler and his conductor friend showed to their class had disappeared and its place had been taken by consumerism, by vulgar consumerism. Of course, that is my assessment, V said, and I was aware that my view might not be shared by others. And I am also aware, V said, that even with his improved standard of living, and technology which allows oneself to improve one's education if one so desires, Stan Butler still would not be able to direct me to the Shakespeare Institute. In that sense, my myth of the England of Shakespeare and the myth of the England of *On the Buses* is not that much of a myth, and the juxtaposition of the two ideas of England is certainly not as absurd as it appeared to some natives when I had told them about it.

As for that question, that question of whether she misses her country, that question, now that the world is fuller of exiles than ever before and so the question does not come up so often, which is a good thing, a very good thing as far as she is concerned, and she knows that question is more to do with people simply parroting what they have heard before and so enabling the world to go on in the same fashion and some people like that the world never changes and that always the same questions are asked but there are those, the likes of Stan Butler among them, those whom it does not suit that the world never changes but they do not seem to realise that it is to their disadvantage that the world never changes and so they too go on asking the same question. But even if they knew that the world never changing is to their disadvantage, V said, would they be able to do anything about it? No, the answer is no, V said. There was a time when such realisations used to upset her and most of her adult life, she said, she wondered why the Stan Butlers of England, as it seemed to her, so willingly accepted their inferior position, their exclusion from the myth of England as the country of Shakespeare and for many years she wished she could do something about it and in some ways she did try to do something, something that went beyond joining demos and protests in the name of this cause or in the name of that cause and in those days she used to think, like some believer in enlightenment, some naïve believer in enlightenment, in improvement, in education, like some naïve believer that she had been for most of her life, but what else could a little girl, a girl who was not yet four, and who had to kneel in a corner of her mother's kitchen and face a blank wall because she could not recite a poem without stumbling and without prompting, for that is the memory of her early childhood, the most abiding memory, what else could she grow up into than a believer in learning, in education that might help those street urchins – the name her mother used to refer to the children who ran around all day long without structured activities – since there was no real education for them, for those Stan Butlers, there were only exams and qualifications, and when she worked in education, she found out that the only thing they cared about were exams and qualification, that was what they were told to want. The exams they passed and the qualifications they gained, that gave them skills enough to read about celebrities in the tabloids, V said at the moment we were approaching the Folly, and these British, grown-up, street urchins are now no different from other, grown-up, street urchins anywhere else in the world and so these days it strikes me, V said, that I am immune to whether the world goes on in the same fashion or not, and so she does not bother with protests, the world can go to hell as far as she is concerned. What interests her is the knowledge that she is different, she has always been different, an exile, born an exile, an exile as an outsider, and being an exile as an outsider is a permanent condition, a much stronger feeling, much stronger than being a geographical exile. Like Marlowe's Mephistopheles, who carries hell within himself and therefore is never out of it regardless of where he goes, she carries her exile inside her, her exile that makes her who she is and so she can never stop being an exile. She is an exile among grown-up, street urchins, she was an exile in her mother's womb, an exile kneeling on the floor in a corner of her mother's kitchen, an exile facing a blank wall, an exile secretly glancing at the horse manure – another name her mother used for street urchins – and exile behind her dark shades, those coloured lenses that all exiles wear permanently, she was an exile thrown into the paddling pool in her nursery by the children who must have been street urchins, all her life she has lived the life of an exile, an exile and an outsider at the same time, an exile among exiles, she said. As for her country, her country in the sense of those who parrot such clichéd sentiments, sometimes she wants to tell them that she needs no country, no country as soil, no country of blood connections, for those are real myths and those are dangerous myths, much more dangerous than the myth of England as the country of Shakespeare and the myth of England as the country of *On the Buses* and so sometimes she wishes to tell them that the only country she needs is her library, her real library and her imaginary library, an ever-expanding, living place of worlds and people, of imaginary places, the library is her world, that's where she desiderates, she said, and perhaps that is why she has never been able to give a book away once she has read it, even when she knew that she would not read it again. And when she travels, that is what she misses, her real library, her books, not countries, mother or father or brother or sister countries. But she does not say that to those who ask, to those who ask whether she misses her country, for anyone who asks such a question does not have a library, does not have a living library. For how could you have a library, a proper library that you have read, that you have read in a way that was meaningful to you and then ask such a question, such a silly question, how could you go on parroting about missing one's country? Let me remind you of the words of Walser, she said, who writes that 'one belongs in the place one longs for'.

At that point we found an empty bench and sat down to ponder in silence the words of the great Swiss.

But those people who ask such questions, V said as we resumed our walk, those people who ask such questions about missing one's country do not think, they do not ask real questions, for the real question would be what are those things that constitute one's country, nor would they think having this country or that country as your country is only a matter of an accident of birth, of being born here or there, or nowhere or everywhere, that it is a matter of being an extravagant stranger of here and nowhere, to paraphrase the description of Othello, that it is a matter of a chance event, and so why bother, why ask? V looked at me at this point as if she had expected me to answer her questions but before I could say anything, she said, as you know, I am only a lodger in this world, I am only a lodger . . . and hardly that, she said and I knew that she was quoting from Ignatius Sancho's letter to Laurence Sterne, where the slave writes in response to a question posed by the author of *Tristram Shandy* on a particular political question of the day. Yes, I am only a lodger . . . and hardly that, Sancho asserts, proudly flaunting his position as an eternal exile, V said.

We reached the park exit at Avenue Ferdousi and parted with a handshake and a kiss on both cheeks, neither French, nor

English. After a few steps, I looked back and saw V's diminishing figure jogging away. The exile, the eternal jogger, my friend V.

The Deal

H E HAD UPSET her. It was about time she told him, she said, that his attitude was hurting her. She was undermined as a woman. Her confidence was seeping away.

He said he didn't want to lose her. He was prepared to do what was necessary. He was prepared to change.

Perhaps she said something or produced a sound, a sign, an exclamation of disbelief.

Yes, people change, people change all the time.

Not at his age. Besides, she didn't want anyone to change, let alone him, she said.

Why not? He didn't want to lose her, he repeated.

It wasn't about losing her. She wasn't going anywhere. What she wished was that he would stop hurting her.

He didn't hear her. Once again, he said he didn't want to lose her. He would change.

She didn't want him to change, she said.

He couldn't win, he complained. She didn't like him as he was and she didn't want him to change. What could he do?

The idea that he would change under pressure from her bothered her. It made her uncomfortable. It made her feel worthless. It made her feel that what he would give her would not be given freely. She wanted him to enjoy the pleasure one experiences choosing a present when there is no obligation to do so. When there is no occasion requiring a present. When one chooses a present for the sake of it. For the pleasure of giving. Then she would have the pleasure of receiving. She longed for that kind of relationship.

Later that day, he sent her a message that he had found a solution that might suit everyone and he would tell her on the phone the next day.

A solution that might suit everyone. Right. Is this a board meeting? A business proposition. How could he be so insensitive? Don't you think he was insensitive, she asked her friend across the small round table. And careless with language, a crime of equal seriousness? A man at the next table looked up. Was she too loud? So what? This man was probably the same. Insensitive. Self-centred. Most of them were.

She waited for her friend to agree. She asked again. Was he insensitive or not? Yes, the friend said, nodding. She wished her friend would be more direct and condemn him.

His message made her angry, she went on. Her first thought was to reply saying she was prepared to offer this and that and in return, as a sort of payment, he should offer this and that. She was going to ask him to sign a contract. But she resisted. She held back until her anger subsided.

Best to meet in person, she wrote, deals clinched on the phone might lead to misunderstanding. She tried to be ironic. She tried to expose his business-speak. He didn't notice.

What bothered her most, she told her friend, was that he didn't seem to consider her feelings. It was all about him, she said. The continual mantra that he didn't want to lose her was irritating. He only thought about himself. He understood nothing of what she said. He understood nothing about her pain.

She knew it was a cliché, but why are men so emotionally illiterate, she asked.

The friend raised her eyebrows and shrugged.

And another thing, she said looking at her friend, he knew nothing about women, this man who grew up with four sisters.

Her anger melted into sadness.

He understood. He accepted responsibility. He was guilty. But she had to give him another chance. Would she? She didn't seem to be prepared to try again.

He was wrong. He had said it. He had said it repeatedly. She was right to complain. He needed that. He needed the kick in the arse. He needed to be woken up. But now that he knew and accepted that he had behaved wrongly, she ought to be gracious and give him another chance.

He would make sure that things were different. He would be more attentive, more considerate of her feelings. He said it and he meant it. But would she give him more time?

Would she? The way she spoke this morning and then that message . . . no, he wasn't hopeful.

He didn't want to lose her. He told her that but she didn't seem to care. She was angry; no doubt about that. She didn't listen to him. He was beginning to wonder whether it was all the same to her what happened to them.

M was right, M was always right. God, he had seen him through enough heartaches. M, dear old M, always ready to offer a metaphorical shoulder to cry on.

But M must know that his advice is unlikely to work. How could he take it easy? Relax. Let time pass and let things settle. Wait for her to calm down. Sit tight through the storm. That's not him. He is the tsar of anxiety. Worry personified. That's him. That's always been him.

Either she will come back, M said, or you will have to get used to life without her.

There must be another option. What if he sent her a note explaining his feelings, admitting his guilt and reiterating how much he would hate to lose her? It is bound to move her. Besides, writing always helps. Helps to clarify his feelings, yes, but would it help the situation? Would it make her see that she had hurt him by calling him insensitive?

It was insensitive of her to call him insensitive.

What happened?

Not much.

Did they carry on seeing each other?

Yes.

Did he change?

No. Not a bit.

And she didn't mind?

Yes, she did.

But she accepted the situation as it was.

Not really.

?

Every now and then she complained. The scenes above were repeated many times.

But nothing changed?

Oh, yes, it did.

?

They died. First one, and then the other.

Love and Doubles

In memory of Ivan Lesiak (1929–2008)

F ROM WHERE I am sitting, I observe a woman. She is slouching in a wicker chair, reading, but her body betrays signs of tension. Every now and then, she looks up from her book. The woman's limbs and shoulders are angular, hard and watchful, as if she were expecting someone, keen not to miss them. Is she waiting for me? The question surprises me. Alert, she raises her head with a sharp movement that causes me to jump. I see a countenance with no smile and eyes that look into the distance, beyond the obvious and through the visible. Young, her face carries no lines. But on her forehead, between her eyebrows, there are twin, vertical shadows. I think of the proof-reader's mark to indicate a new paragraph. For now, they are undiscernible to her and those who know her. But I can see them. I know the space between her eyebrows has been reserved for the worry lines which, I feel uncannily certain, will indent themselves in years to come. But how can I be a prophet of her face, of the changes it is to undergo?

The shoulder-length hair is straight and light-honey colour-ed. I continue to stare at her, hoping she won't notice. I rec-ognise the book. I have the same edition of Calvino's *If on a Winter's Night* but my copy is more battered than the one she is holding. Like me, she folds the spine of the book and I know she is a reader, rather than a pedant bothered about preserving a pristine copy. When, after some time, she tucks her hair behind her ears, using her fingers as a brush, I forget myself and make an involuntary exclamation. She turns round and I fear I have been discovered. I bite my lips. Why do I fear her noticing me? And why am I relieved when she fails to look in my direction? A man walks towards her, she speaks to him and I hear anxiety in her words, words that are louder than is necessary for a conversation with someone in such close proximity. Soon, she checks herself or maybe her voice softens in response to what he says. A realisation comes to me, slowly, like the zoom on a camera lens. She is me. My younger self. My never-existing sister. My long-lost double. My like-ness. No wonder she simultaneously intrigues and unsettles me. She is the other, my missing half, the other I have been hoping to find for many years, wondering whether they would be male, female or neither, or both; whether they would be alive or dead. For a split-second, I experience the warmth of hope, of arrival even, of certainty of oneness, that comforting moment, self-deceiving or not, the moment when the world makes sense, when you feel you have come home to the other, whom you do not know but who is no more a stranger to you than you are to yourself. But the feeling of recognition is not as overwhelming or as moving as I had imagined it would be. Within moments, my chest tightens: I have no reason to rejoice. I have to accept that this discovery is too late. He has found her first and claimed her as his other.

Sorrow settles on me like a hungry scavenger. My inner self cries silently. What now? What can I do now that I know she is there but walk away? It is early morning and I begin to wonder whether she is part of a nightmare, a ghost, a cher-ished fantasy turned into a dream, or a memory from many yesterdays ago.

You can never step into the same river twice.

Don't walk away, I tell myself. So what if he loves her? You can love her too. And she can love you. Your shared double.

In the days that follow, I continue to observe them. After a fortnight, I am familiar with their habitual haunts, their times of day, their days of the week, and I find myself shamefully obsessed with her. When I don't see her, thoughts of her occupy my waking hours. I watch them at a concert where she accompanies him, I learn, because he asks her, not because she is interested in the music. But why does she do that? I want her to be herself. She forever compromises, letting her life pass by without being who she wishes to be. Is she doing it for love? Is that what people do for love? There is no doubt that she is loved by the man who was with her when I first saw her, and by many others. But none of them is her true double. With true doubles there is no need for compromise. Why settle for a non-double and compromise?

I make a different choice.

I go on another quest.

In the office to collect my students' essays on the significance of Baudrillard's concept of simulacrum, I watch Professor P leaning over the photocopier. My mind is still preoccupied with the woman. I look at the Professor, who is sufficiently self-centred to be oblivious of the world, perhaps eccentric, or focused on a task at hand, in that single-minded way that I associate with men, who presses his nose against the glass panel, lowers the cover as far as it will go over his head and, like some huge trapped insect, waves his right arm in the air until his hand locates the start button. As soon as he presses it, a darkly smudged sheet with the outline of his face rolls out of the machine. He picks it up, chuckles to himself, still unaware of the world, and walks away whistling a tune, his body bobbing to the rhythm. A smug old man. I busy myself in the office, furtively glancing towards the secretary. She will leave soon; her lunch hour is approaching.

Self-conscious, I wait to be alone before I push my face on the glass of the photocopier, listen for the sound of any approaching steps, and then press the button. The machine groans and stops. An LED indicates that it is jammed. The glass display instructs me to open compartments four and five. I do. I pull out the offending sheets. The light is still flashing. I repeat the process, wondering, as I usually do when poking around inside a photocopier, whether my fingers might touch a live wire and I might electrocute myself. Sometimes I even feel tempted by this possibility, not because I am suicidal, but because the notion of the unexpected and spectacular amuses me. I picture my body histrionically sprawled in front of the machine and the next user having to push me out of the way before doing their copying. I think of the people who would find the image of my face, fixed by the photocopier. At the memorial service they would probably mention the image as a sign of . . . what? My sense of humour. Of course, only in the spirit of *de mortuis nil nisi bonum*. They might pass a copy of my image around, or even project it on PowerPoint. The thought that I was desperate for the other and that my life-long quest, supported by my unshakeable belief in the platonic story of love, led me to mock the idea by making a black and white simulacrum, a photocopied image of the me who, lost in time, the me who is no more, that thought might cross the minds of my colleagues but their sense of decorum at the occasion would prevail and they would not voice such thoughts. It was an accident, they would say of my death, and to lighten the tone they could have the image printed on a memorial card to be distributed at the wake. It would be my last message to the world; a posthumously released image then becomes my definitive image. The idea makes me smile.

Faced with the broken photocopier, I ignore my fears, as I have done many times before, thinking, foolishly perhaps, that since I have survived so many similar occasions, nothing should happen this time. I repeat the action as instructed. As soon as the machine is back in order, I try again: my face pressed firmly against the glass. A sheet rolls out. Black. Evenly black all over. I hold it against the light. No outline of my face. I throw the sheet in the recycling bin. I move to try again but the photocopier flashes a sign indicating that it is out of toner.

I walk away and remember B. We were brought together by a machine like this one. He gave me a photocopy of an article on critical theory, our shared passion at the time – cannot remember which one it was . . . Tony Bennett's perhaps, or could it have been J Hillis-Miller's musings on the figure in the carpet? – and, seeing that I was pleased, asked me out. In days to come, we read Borges in bed on the abominations of mirrors, which, like fatherhood, procreate images of us, and wonder why the great Argentinean never mentioned photo-copiers. When things are going well and we lie in each other's arms, B says that he wants to thank that photocopier. And how appropriate, we think, that in our age of copies, of mass production, of nothing original under the sun (as Beckett's *Murphy* says, 'The sun shone, having no alternative, on the nothing new'), duplicating machines generate love affairs and possibly procreations too. Abominable, Jorge Luis might have said. However, when it all ends disastrously, I do not blame the photocopier. I don't know about B. Sometimes I ask myself, and the thought still amuses me, years after we parted, whether he approaches these machines with trepidation.

Today, I wonder whether a photocopier, or better still, a 3-D printer, could produce a double? An exact replica? A fixed double or a double for every day of our lives. The ultimate proliferation and abomination.

Or, in what seems to be a nightmare scenario, as far removed from Diotima's story as it is possible to be, you can always be cloned. A perfect, useless, phoney double, more double than a double. Love your double, love yourself, your secret sharer.

A day after he photocopied his face, Professor P dies unexpectedly, in his sleep. His seminar on twins in *The Comedy of Errors*, due the following day, and which I was to attend, is cancelled.

What happened to the image?

I ask the secretary to lend me the key to the Professor's office. His desk is always covered with piles of documents but perhaps I could quickly search for the photocopy.

'He told me last week that he had added comments on a thesis he was helping me supervise,' I lie to the secretary. 'It must be in the office.'

The secretary takes the key from a drawer in the cabinet next to her and is about to hand it to me but then changes her mind: 'I will come with you; there is something I need too.'

I have to abandon my plan. The secretary enters first and laughs. Professor P's photocopied face greets us from the wall opposite the door, ensconced in a baroque, golden frame. My turn to laugh: his image is smiling, a rakish, ironic smile. But that's not all. The Professor's desk is empty expect for a neat stack of students' essays in one corner. Had he planned it?

Once upon a time (and what a time it was) in a far away country (it had to be another country, but the wench is not dead, contrary to what Barabas claimed) on a late afternoon, I enter an art gallery in the city centre. It is the opening night of a group show. As is usual on such occasions, the place is teeming with fashionably dressed men and women, clinking their white-wine glasses, talking loudly, while casually bumping into one another and kissing, the European way, on both cheeks. I'm all alone, isolated in my simple, navy-blue coat, a colour which is not in fashion that season, but is like a uniform, a second skin to me, and jotting down a poem which I, a serious, bookish seventeen-year-old, have been composing in my head. I am not aware of it at the time but it will occur to me later that I would have been the only person in the gallery who was surrounded by so much space. A shadow falls on my poem. Annoyed at the interruption, I stop writing and look up. He is short with a lively face and eyes which are both serious and teasing, both raffish and innocent. I wait for him to speak. The fact that he is a generation older than me gives me confidence. He goes straight to the point and invites me to visit him in his studio.

Was there a sense of recognition on his part when he stood in front of me? Was it the feeling that his possible double was standing in a corner that made him abandon others and join me? These are questions that occur to me now, not then. But I know that when I climbed the stairs that led to his studio a few days after the vernissage, I walked in the hope, no matter how faint or impossible, that the man might be my double, the long-lost double whose interests and preoccupations would match my own in the way that adjoining jigsaw pieces inter-link to create a smooth surface with no bumps. In my youth, not only did I believe in Diotima's story of love but I made an effort, whenever I sensed a chance of a double, to find them.

How do the lucky ones find their doubles? Assuming that happens. Do they experience an epiphany: a sure proof that they have found their other half (or so they think, for a while, at least)? The lucky ones who do not need years of getting to know each other, years of holding back and allowing the other to peel away the outer casing, layer by layer at decent inter-vals. Oh, those phoney, time-wasting delays! Strategies and excuses. Games and face-saving tricks. Deliberately overloaded time-tables and responses like 'I need to check my diary'. How many times have I heard that? And said it, too, in response to those I didn't care to meet but who might have thought I was their double. We are all guilty. All hypocrites. What a waste! And then we talk of love, all that to get us through, to paper over our doubts!

His studio is on a hill above the city, an excellent place to take refuge from the lives down below. We talk a great deal. Each of us has a turn. We look at his art, take time thinking about it. We read together. Poems, philosophy, narratives. We are doubles. Our minds and bodies fit together.

On my own, I read the books he recommends. He recites his poetry and I listen.

One day he tells me off for wearing fashionable platforms. Is that because he recognises the first crack in his belief (a self-delusion?)? Is he annoyed, because he cannot accept that he was wrong? Is he annoyed because he knows he is running out of time and energy to seek a double? It may be easier to cheat a bit and overlook whatever does not fit (but no, he cannot do that, he is a perfectionist).

Perhaps, he is not my double. It only appeared so to both of us because, as a teenager in awe, and in love, I am pliable.

Perhaps he thought he could mould me in the image of his double that exists in his imagination, or, if you believe Plato, in his memory?

He says I am becoming like the rest of the crowd. I know I am not. I don't tell him that I need to try out different ways of being myself so that I have some idea who I want to be. He guesses my thoughts and says that there is no time to waste trying different ways. Most of them don't lead anywhere. 'Trust me,' he says.

He takes me to see *Andrei Rublev*, a film about the great icon painter. A master of images.

'He was serious about his art,' my friend says as we walk home.

'He was a monk,' I retort.

'An artist has to be a monk,' he says. I know he only half-believes what he says. I don't need to remind him that, affected by the atrocities around him, Rublev temporarily loses his ability to paint, inadvertently chooses life over art.

When the sun is out, we sunbathe. And think. And dream. He is Diogenes, he says. But as an artist, his god is Apollo. I should be serious about my work, he insists.

I am fascinated by him; in my teenage ardour I even think that I adore him, but he is not a god. He is a sculptor and I must guard against him becoming my Pygmalion. I dislike that male-centred story. I am a woman who will fashion herself in the image of her own choosing.

I stop seeing him for a while, for two years exactly, and

only go back when I know for sure what kind of shoes I want to wear, when I love and admire him but am no longer meek to speak out and defend my choice, whatever it is. And when I learn to criticise Picasso, without reciting what I am told to think.

We are lovers for a year when one day I make my way to his studio to tell him that I am leaving the country. He doesn't ask why so I say I need to find my own space outside the rules of my family, my nationality and class. (Unlike Stephen Dedalus, whose words I was probably echoing, consciously or unconsciously, I do not need to add religion to the list of nets I wish to escape.) Today the words sound like a poem, or even a slogan learned by heart. But I did believe in them then as I do now.

He says what he is hearing from me is the empty rhetoric of youth and that it is irrelevant where we live. All that matters is to be serious about one's work. I am too excited about my decision to react in any other way but to smile. In many ways, I have already left.

A year later I revisit the country and the sculptor. He is glad to see me, but not overwhelmed. We talk about the year we have spent apart. Half way through my visit, he stands up and says that he has to show me something. He reappears carrying a shoe box. He holds it on his lap, gently lifts the lid and takes out a sheet of photographic paper. He passes it on to me without saying a word. I am looking at thirty-six tiny shots, arranged in four rows. The box contains several hundred sheets, thousands of pictures. Shot one after another. Placed on a roll and moved quickly in front of the viewer's eyes, the figure would appear animated. The figure of one and the same woman: me.

'Think,' he says, 'we are all connected across space and time.'

What about memory? Memory of the time when we were whole.

We sit next to each other as he hands me one sheet after another. I take them and peer closely at the images. I want to ask questions but I know they cannot be answered. Silent, we think our separate thoughts.

Who took the pictures? When? Where? Why, on some of them, am I looking straight into the camera and yet I have no recollection of the event? I have never seen the surroundings. I have never worn those clothes. But perhaps those are details I may not have noticed at the time. All of this is irrelevant. What bothers me, and amuses me, however, is the sheer quantity of the images. It suggests obsession on his part. But then, in my language, obsession is the sister of passion. I both fear and desire obsessions and passions.

I am puzzled and confused. He says he knows what I am thinking. I may not believe it, but the pictures are not of me. I learn that she is someone whom he met at the seaside last summer. Yes, the resemblance is uncanny – the same honey-coloured hair, angular shape with a touch of tension in her shoulders – that was precisely what drew him towards her in the crowd. Moreover, her voice was like mine, usually too loud. Was her mind like mine? I wonder. He does not know. He cannot tell. He had talked to her about me, 'incessantly, I fear,' he says, 'and she listened. During the fortnight that we spent together, days and nights, she might have begun to live you,' he adds.

'She was your double, an ideal double as far as I am concerned. She played your part better than you. She let me love her. She promised she would never leave me. That's all she wanted, having my love and loving me.'

But that could not be enough.

'Yes, she fitted too well,' he says with a sigh, holding back his tears.

But that's not the kind of double I long for. What he is seeking is a replacement. A replica, a copy of me. She was my visual double on which he wrote his desires. He moulded and created a woman only to find her too perfect.

What I am seeking in the other is emotional and intellectual accordance with me.

'Perhaps, she was a devil, a ghost.'

Why does he say that?

He is aware of my thoughts.

'Since parting with her, I have written but received no answers to my letters. I travelled to her part of the country, but the address did not exist.'

He has scoured colleges, places where young people meet, visited areas where people gather, talked to anyone he could find in the small town, even checked the national register. The last search came up with seven women of the same name. He has traced them all; none of them was her. And yet he knew that her name was not invented. He had seen her passport, heard her parents speak to her on the phone.

Perhaps she was a ghost, existing only in his mind. I don't tell him that.

'And,' he says, standing and looking very serious, 'I have these photographs to prove that I knew her. You cannot take pictures of someone who exists only in your mind, no matter how well you focus the lens,' he says.

Mindful of his grief, I don't say that only a fool trusts images.

Back in my hotel room, my mind is buzzing with questions: could the pictures have been of me? Over the years he photographed me several times. Is it reasonable to assume that I cannot recall every single one of those occasions? Or, because she could only exist as my double and now that I am back, and he is not overwhelmed at the prospect, he does not need either of us. After all, he has all those images. They matter to an artist. And he is a sculptor. He could breathe life into them. Isn't that what every man would like to do?

I realise with sadness that in all this pandemonium of absurdity and randomness, reality and fiction, there are three lost solitary beings: her, him and me.

Many years have passed since the scenes on the terrace and the pictures in the shoe box. Occasionally I think of those hundreds of photographs. Should I have made copies of them? I know that my memory of what happened is possibly correct, possibly confused, but I accept it as such.

At my age, I find it reassuring to look at old pictures and remember the past, the past when I was someone with a future, someone who believed in the story of the double. It helps me assuage the anxiety, the growing fear that one morning I may look in my bathroom mirror and see nothing but the tiles covering the wall opposite.

Will all my hopes be lost when that happens? Maybe I will have this story, this impalpable and protecting mist of memory, to rely upon and to hold onto as a proof that I existed, with or without a double.

Last year on a holiday in Marienbad, I walked through the

hotel's immaculately kept gardens, half-listening to a man, an elegantly dressed and coiffed man who looked like any other nearby, and who followed me around telling me that we had met before. He described past occasions, often dwelling on details, when we spent time together, but, despite all his efforts, I knew we had never met before. I let him join me on my walks because I could see that he believed in what he was saying. He was the same age as me, but in terms of the travel and the quest, he was at an earlier stage of the journey.

I, however, have moved on. Since the events described in what you have just read, my quest for a double, if you can still call it a quest for a double, has taken another form. After all, doubles, like husbands and lovers, like the women in 'The Love Song of J Alfred Prufrock', come and go. These days my doubles exist as unattainable longings, fixed in the past or future, rather like the love between the lovers on Keats' urn, or sometimes my doubles appear as fleeting memories, recollections of something that may or may not have happened.

Here is one of those: I am twenty-three years old, sitting at a table in a Bloomsbury pub with Alan, my boyfriend of that summer in London. I still have a copy of *The Princeton Encyclopaedia of Poetry and Poetics* that he gave me then. He is an American, a draft dodger, 'an angel from the city of angels', as he keeps reminding me. Hardly, but that's no matter. He talks and talks and I listen without following what he is saying. Behind his shoulder, I see a face. She is in her thirties, bottle blond. Her straw-like hair frames a face with heavily made-up eyes, strong dark eyebrows and red lipstick. Her customer, for there is no doubt about his role, is talking to her, his hand on the woman's fleshy thigh, exposed by a miniskirt ridden high. Our eyes meet and she smiles at me. I smile back, secure in the knowledge that, at that moment, no one and nothing else exists except the two of us, and our understanding. For that fragile moment, she is my double, the other I love. The other who loves me. The other who holds up a mirror to me. The other in whom I catch a fleeting glimpse of who I am. A lost woman, bored with the man next to me but hoping, always hoping.

And then, as is bound to happen, the gods intervene and for whatever sins we have committed, they separate us, toss us around and we begin another quest.

Today the memory makes me think of Roland Barthes writing that 'life consists of these little touches of solitude', occasionally shared, broken.

Doubles are illusions. Doubles are imaginary. I know that now. I try another way of finding the other, the mirror, the love, myself.

I develop a passion for solitude and I try to live without my life depending on love. I write. I write, *donc je suis*. But I exist only for a moment, fleeting and fragile. I am I only for a moment. Fleeting and fragile.

I write. *Donc je suis.* That is my way to continue, even pointlessly to keep going to postpone the anxiety awaiting me when I stop.

What do I write? My stories are collages of borrowed and stolen words, overheard and overused, phrases and sentences lifted from the crowd. I copy them from others and write them down as my own. After all, can there possibly be anything that isn't a copy? In the end, one is always writing one's own writing, doubling up on oneself. In the end, one is always writing about love. In the end, I have to fool myself that my writing is a quest for a double rather than a quest for vanity and void.

You, hypocrite reader, my likeness, my secret sharer, my double.

A Love Song for MJL

THE ENCORE OVER, the applause dies down. She stands up and puts on her coat. Without looking at me. He, the man at the end of the row – her husband? – speaks to her. They are ready to leave. There is still hope. Or not? That's how it happens. Eyes to eyes. Silent. On a train. In a crowd. At a theatre. Meaningful. Yes. The other has found you. You have found the other. But then . . . but then . . . it's no more than a fleeting interest. A precursory glance, a tease to help us see out the day.

The other has found you. You, the gullible one. Forever gullible. You, the hopeful one. Hopeful against hope. Hopeful against experience.

The other has found you. Not these days. Not when you're three score and ten.

She picks up the programme. Her programme. Her programme she has shared with me. Was that all? Kindness. Kindness and nothing else.

But kindness is all.

She offers the programme to me without a word. Do I want it? Silence, broken by her voice:

Are you a musician?

No.

An artist?

No.

My companions are ready. My wife is aware I am talking

to the woman. The woman is aware my wife is ready to leave. The woman says.

I would like to see you again.

Is that what she says? Yes.

I would like to see you again.

I hear urgency in her words.

Has she got an email?

She writes it down.

A week later, the crumpled piece of paper is still in my pocket. I keep turning it round with the tips of my fingers. It's a paper ball now. Our globe.

Do I dare disturb the universe? I am an old fool (even if not an attendant lord).

Do I dare disturb the universe?

Yes.

Yes?

Let us go before the eternal footman holds my coat and snickers. I am afraid but let us go. You and I.

Acknowledgements

Thank you to Salt for believing in me.

Thank you to John Oakey for his patience and imagination in designing the cover.

Thank you to Nicholas Royle for suggesting the collection and for his sensitive and painstaking editing.

Thank you to my daughters, Rebecca and Hannah Partos, for their love and inspiration.

Thank you to Peter Main, my first reader, for his help and support, and for putting up with me.

Thank you to Anthony Rudolf for his insight, generosity and friendship.

NEW FICTION FROM SALT

RON BUTLIN
Billionaires' Banquet (978-1-78463-100-0)

NEIL CAMPBELL
Sky Hooks (978-1-78463-037-9)

SUE GEE
Trio (978-1-78463-061-4)

CHRISTINA JAMES
Rooted in Dishonour (978-1-78463-089-8)

V.H. LESLIE
Bodies of Water (978-1-78463-071-3)

WYL MENMUIR
The Many (978-1-78463-048-5)

ALISON MOORE
Death and the Seaside (978-1-78463-069-0)

ANNA STOTHARD
The Museum of Cathy (978-1-78463-082-9)

STEPHANIE VICTOIRE
The Other World, It Whispers (978-1-78463-085-0)

RECENT FICTION FROM SALT

This book has been typeset by
SALT PUBLISHING LIMITED
using Neacademia, a font designed by Sergei Egorov
for the Rosetta Type Foundry in the Czech Republic.
It is manufactured using Creamy 70gsm, a Forest
Stewardship Council™ certified paper from Stora Enso's
Anjala Mill in Finland. It was printed and bound by
Clays Limited in Bungay, Suffolk, Great Britain.

LONDON
GREAT BRITAIN
MMXVIII